"Are you okay?" he asked.

Was that a trace of amusement she heard in his voice? Squinting, she saw the kick of his lips, the warmth in his eyes. "What's so funny?"

"You look like a walking, breathing dust mite," Muzi said, his laughter flowing over her. Oh, yeah, his smile could power the sun. And beneath his short beard, she saw the hint of two sexy dimples. Dimples were her kryptonite...

"And you have spiderwebs in your hair," he pointed out.

"Do you think they are all gone?" Ro asked from behind her curtain of hair.

She felt his fingers in her hair, a long curl sliding across his hand. "Yep."

Ro tossed her hair back and met his eyes, dark, deep and oh so intense.

Later on, she would ask herself who made the first move, him or her. But now, in a fraction of a second, his lips were on hers, his hand found her lower back and he pulled her into his big, strong, hard-everywhere body. Her hand curled around the back of his strong neck and his mouth tasted like peppermint and coffee. In his arms, she felt safe and secure, protected.

South Africa's Scandalous Billionaires

First comes scandal, then comes marriage...?

Radd and Digby Tempest-Vane are South Africa's youngest billionaires and they'll do anything to rebuild their family's empire! Their reputations might be infamous, but they'll be put to the test when two complicated women explode into their world...

But not before they get the biggest shock of all— there's another secret Tempest-Vane heir!

Powerful Radd's instant connection with shy florist Brinley Riddell may cause him to risk it all when her past threatens to destroy his plans!

Read Radd and Brin's story in
How to Undo the Proud Billionaire

Digby has a vision for his family's hotel and it's *very* specific. Interior designer and single mother Bay Adaire beats all of his expectations, but breaking down her walls won't be easy!

Discover Digby and Bay's story in
How to Win the Wild Billionaire

Reluctant to take on her billion-dollar birthright, Roisin escapes to her newly inherited vineyard. And invites her brother's best friend, Muzi Miya-Matthews...

Check out Muzi and Roisin's story in
How to Tempt the Off-Limits Billionaire

All available now!

Joss Wood

HOW TO TEMPT THE OFF-LIMITS BILLIONAIRE

PRESENTS

ISBN-13: 978-1-335-56807-6

How to Tempt the Off-Limits Billionaire

Copyright © 2021 by Joss Wood

Harlequin Enterprises ULC
22 Adelaide St. West, 40th Floor
Toronto, Ontario M5H 4E3, Canada
www.Harlequin.com

Printed in U.S.A.

Recycling programs
for this product may
not exist in your area.

Joss Wood loves books and traveling—especially to the wild places of southern Africa and, well, anywhere. She's a wife, a mom to two teenagers and a slave to two cats. After a career in local economic development, she now writes full-time. Joss is a member of Romance Writers of America and Romance Writers of South Africa.

Books by Joss Wood

Harlequin Presents

South Africa's Scandalous Billionaires

How to Undo the Proud Billionaire
How to Win the Wild Billionaire

Harlequin Desire

Hot Holiday Fling

Murphy International

One Little Indiscretion
Temptation at His Door
Back in His Ex's Bed

Visit the Author Profile page
at Harlequin.com for more titles.

CHAPTER ONE

Hey, gorgeous, if you're looking for that pretty pink thong, you left it at my place last night. I'm sitting at my desk, it's in my pocket, and I keep remembering how I slid it down your hips…

ROISIN FROWNED, TRYING to make sense of the words when another message popped up on her screen.

You there? Huh, you must be busy. Anyway, just wanted you to know that I had the best time!

Her fingers hit the keyboard with more force than necessary. I'm so glad you had fun, she typed.

FYI, I'm halfway across the world, you cheating scumbag!

Now, sitting on one of the backless, effortlessly sexy couches in the lobby of The Vane hotel, the luxurious hotel owned by her biological brothers, Roisin O'Keefe scrolled through the text messages she'd exchanged with Kelvin since he'd, inadvertently, let the cat out of the bag.

It was an accident. I didn't mean for it to happen.

Yeah, sure. The "accident" defense was old and tired and didn't work because people weren't prone to randomly falling—naked—into other people's arms, and beds.

We've been together since college. You can't just throw us away, Ro!

No, *he'd* thrown *them* away when he decided to play Remove-Her-Panties with the owner of the pretty pink thong.

Kelvin's infidelity hurt—of course it did, she wasn't a robot—but Ro knew that her heart wasn't completely broken. Maybe just a little battered, slightly bruised?

And, under the occasional prickles of pain, there was relief. A lot of it.

And that was partly because she no longer felt obligated to tell her boyfriend that she'd inherited almost a billion dollars from her biological parents a few months before.

She'd dreaded breaking the life-changing news to Kelvin. As a financial advisor, he would've insisted on taking control of the situation, demanding that she let him act as her business representative. He would've freaked at her insistence on giving most of her windfall away and urged her to buy property, shares, upgrade her house, and her car. And *his* house and *his* car. After six years together, and much prodding, he'd finally proposed and she'd spent the next two years nagging him to set a wedding date. Ro had no doubt that, given her change of fortune, he'd want them marrying right away.

Having access to a billion dollars was a hell of an incentive to marry...

She'd initially felt guilty at her cynical thoughts but now, many weeks after her leaving Los Angeles, she knew her instincts about her long-term partner were right. Kelvin was fundamentally, and sadly, untrustworthy.

Pink thong girl was welcome to him.

Another reason to thank the gods she'd kept her life-changing news to herself—she had yet to tell anyone, not even her adoptive parents, about her inheritance—was she knew that, had she told Kelvin and then broken up with him, he wouldn't have hesitated to sell her story to the highest bidder.

And it was a hell of a story. After birthing three sons and plundering one of Africa's oldest and wealthiest family-owned business, the uber-moneyed and infamous South African powerhouse couple, Gil and Zia Tempest-Vane, found themselves pregnant with baby number four. Uninterested in raising another child—not that they'd given their other three children much attention—they gave her, their only daughter, up for adoption in the USA and immediately returned to their licentious lives jet-setting around the world.

For the best part of the next three decades, they frequently hit the headlines and there wasn't a vice they weren't intimately acquainted with: drugs, orgies, infidelities and bad behavior were routinely covered by the international press. Sadly, not even the death of their son tamped down their pleasure-seeking instincts.

Jack was the oldest of Ro's biological brothers and, from what she'd learned, had been an exceptional young man. Whip-smart, athletic and, according to Radd and Digby, responsible, caring and soul-deep honorable. His death from a brain aneurysm shortly after his twenty-first birthday devastated his brothers. Jack was their guiding light, hero and role model. Their rock throughout their tumultuous childhoods.

Jack's death, and Gil and Zia's lack of grief, were the catalysts for Radd and Digby to emotionally, and permanently, divorce themselves from their parents.

Ro couldn't blame them for that. Gil and Zia's domination of the social pages and gossip columns continued unabated. Their deaths in a horrific car accident in California two years ago left a hole in the news cycle and that hole was partly filled by the incessant speculation of who would inherit their enormous estate.

As far as the world knew, Gil and Zia only brought three boys into the world—Jack, Radd and Digby. Nobody knew about their fourth child as Ro's birth and adoption were well-kept secrets. But when they died, Ro, who'd always known she was adopted, learned that she was *their* child—their sole beneficiary, in fact—and that she had two biological brothers.

Right now, nobody could link Ro O'Keefe, American kindergarten teacher, with Gil and Zia Tempest-Vane. And if the press discovered her connection to them, the internet would explode. She would be front-page news worldwide and hounded wherever she went.

That didn't sound like fun.

Ro flipped her phone from hand to hand, thinking that, at some point, she'd have to tell her adoptive parents about her inheritance, but they had their issues they were currently working through. Issues she was also trying to make sense of...

After a thirty-five-year relationship, one adopted child, and a supposedly rock-solid and indestructible marriage, her parents were talking divorce, telling her that they'd drifted apart and now wanted different things and, maybe—*bleurgh*—different people.

As a result, Ro couldn't help questioning her beliefs about love, commitment and marriage. She'd genuinely believed her parents were perfectly matched, the best of friends who enjoyed a happy, passionate marriage.

No wonder she was confused about love and what it was supposed to be. Until she could make sense of the concept, she intended to avoid men and relationships.

Ro glanced at her watch, thinking that she had a

little time before she was due to meet Radd and Digby on the back lawn of their six-star hotel. In summer, when the bright days slid into light, balmy evenings, the hotel staff served sundowners and cocktails to the guests sitting under the huge oak trees dominating the wide swathe of bright green lawn. The fragrance from the graduated rose garden—white to pink to red blooms—drifted over the prosperous guests lounging in comfortable deck chairs and on outdoor settees, content to listen to a string quartet play the classics while watching the light changing on Table Mountain, the famous Cape Town landmark looming over the hotel.

The Vane had recently been voted one of the best hotels in the world, and Ro was proud of her brothers. They'd worked so hard to make the hundred-year-old hotel—one of the many business enterprises they owned—a destination venue.

It was strange to think that her biological parents had met in this hotel, were married in the chapel on the grounds, had their wedding reception in the opulent ballroom upstairs. It was odd to think of Gil and Zia at all, and she was still wrapping her head around the fact that she carried the genes of the world's most famous decadent couple.

Ro crossed her legs and looked down at the harlequin floor, feeling, as she frequently did, like she was standing in a small bucket on a storm-tossed ocean.

Six months ago, she lived a normal, very middle-class life. She worked as a kindergarten teacher, had an active social life with Kelvin, had lunch dates with her girlfriends and juggled the bills every month. Now, in a foreign country and far away from her support structure, she relied on her brothers and their fiancées for support and friendship.

And, thanks to a bulging portfolio of property, art, cars, stock and cash, she was ridiculously, stupendously, insanely wealthy. With one call to the trust's lawyers, she could have tens of millions of dollars transferred to her account and she could buy anything, anywhere, at any time.

Like many people, she'd dreamed of winning the lottery but, honestly, abruptly acquiring a fortune wasn't nearly as much fun as she'd expected it to be.

It should be simple but it wasn't, especially since she had to keep her identity a secret. On hearing about her parentage and inheritance, she'd traveled to Cape Town and applied for a job at The Vane hotel. She had wanted to learn about her biological brothers before revealing who she was, thinking that if she didn't like them, she was under no obligation, legal or otherwise, to reveal their connection.

Digby, on hearing that she was a kindergarten teacher, hired her to look after Olivia, his interior decorator's niece, so that Bay could renovate certain rooms of this hotel. She'd come to know Digby, then Radd, and on finding them as lovely and honorable as Jack was reputed to be, revealed that she was their sister.

But they were the only people who knew and, as a kindergarten teacher and an ex-employee of this hotel, she couldn't be seen tossing money around like confetti without attracting questions and attention.

"Ro-Ro!"

Ro jerked her head up, a smile hitting her face as she watched one of her favorite people in the world, a two-foot-high fairy, barrel across the lobby toward her, pigtails bouncing.

Livvie threw herself into her arms and Ro caught her, swinging her up onto her knee and returning the little girl's rambunctious hug. Over her sweet-smelling head, Ro scanned the lobby, looking for Bay or Digby, Liv's soon-to-be parents. She didn't see either, but she did see Tall, Dark, Ripped and Handsome—dressed in chino shorts and a white expensive linen shirt—heading in her direction.

Ro's gaze slammed into his, her breath hitched and her stomach was invaded by a colony of squirrels on speed. She felt the heat in her cheeks and her womb, and the world faded as the man, six-four, muscles on muscles, headed her way. Her eyes drifted over him, taking in his designer clothes and the sleek watch on his strong wrist. It might be, she suspected, a limited edition Patek Philippe. Or something else ridiculously expensive and exceedingly rare.

He was a study in black and brown, rich, luscious and lovely...

Warm brown skin, black eyes, high cheekbones and a closely cropped beard. Then his eyes moved to Livvie and blindingly white, even teeth flashed as he smiled.

Ro grabbed the edge of the bench, hoping she

wouldn't tumble to the floor. She couldn't—not only was she holding Livvie, but she'd also make a fool of herself in front of some of the world's most discerning guests.

She shouldn't be fascinated by anyone, Ro told herself, her thoughts frantic. She was nursing a battered heart, her life was a mess, she had decisions to make and she did not need the complication of being attracted to a sexy, stunning man.

"You must be Roisin," he said when he stopped a few feet from them. His voice was deep, dark and sinful, and Ro felt her skin prickle.

"It's Ro*sheen*, actually, but I prefer to be called Ro," she corrected him as she stood up. She took a deep breath and held out her hand for him to shake. "And you are?"

"Muzi Miya-Matthews," he said, his huge hand swallowing hers. "I'm a very old friend of Digby's."

Her head swam and she took a deep breath, not wanting him to know how much he affected her.

What had they been talking about? Ah, right. He was the wine entrepreneur and CEO; she'd heard Dig mention him.

"I would've thought we would cross paths before," Muzi said, sliding his hands into the pockets of his chinos, the action pulling his shirt tight across his acre-wide chest, "but life has been a little hectic lately."

Ro stroked Livvie's thigh. He ran, she recalled, one of the oldest premier wine and spirits companies in the country and was regarded as one of the country's best vintners. Muzi Miya-Matthews was a force to be reckoned with in the wine industry, so she had to wonder why he was babysitting Olivia. Especially when Digby and Bay knew that they could call on her, and did, whenever they needed childcare help.

She raised her eyebrows. "You and Livvie?"

Muzi held out his hands and Livvie tumbled from Ro's arms into his, squealing when Muzi pretended to drop her. Actually, it was Ro who squealed. Livvie just laughed.

Muzi looked at her, obviously amused, as he held Livvie like he would a rugby ball, tucked under his arm. "Sorry, it's a game we play, the girl is fearless."

Yep, she knew that. Looking after Livvie required an eagle eye. Or ten. "Bay has only been in Digby's life for a couple of months, but you two seem to have a strong connection?"

Hey, she was a teacher, it was her job to be suspicious.

"Digby is my best friend and I'm tight with his family," Muzi replied, running his big hand over Livvie's head. "Digby has known my grandmother Mimi forever and Bay and Mimi have struck up a friendship. I was inspecting the vineyards next to Mimi's house today and Liv and Bay were there, lunching with her. Liv walked a part of Mimi's vineyard with me and Mimi's dogs while Bay and my grandmother chatted. Bay needed to see a client on the other side of the city this afternoon, so I offered to hand Liv over to Digby." He rubbed his right ear and grimaced. "She talked nonstop for the hour-long journey back."

Ah, okay. That made sense.

Ro watched as Liv rubbed her eyes and before she could tell Muzi that the little girl was exhausted, he took her and propped her on his hip. Liv immediately rested her head on his chest, eyes fluttering closed. Liv never seemed to run out of energy so seeing her fade was a surprise. "How much walking did she do?" Ro asked.

"A lot," Muzi told her. "She felt morally obligated to keep up with Mimi's dogs."

Muzi adjusted the pink backpack on his shoulder and lifted his chin in the direction of the wide French doors that led onto a wraparound veranda. "Digby messaged me to meet him on the back lawn. I presume you are heading in that direction?"

Ro nodded. "Yes, I'm having afternoon drinks with my—"

Ro stopped abruptly, shocked that she'd almost told this man that Digby and Radd were her brothers. The fact that she was Zia and Gil's natural daughter, and that she'd inherited their extensive estate, was highly classified information. If her identity became public knowledge, her life would become intolerable.

"I know that you are Digby and Radd's sister, Ro."

Ro stared at him, her heart in her throat and dread rolling over her. "How do you know that? Nobody knows that!"

Muzi placed his hand on her lower back and gently pushed her out of the way of a group of Italian women, exquisitely dressed. "Digby and I have been best friends since we were thirteen. He knows all my secrets and I know his."

Ro squeezed her eyes together, tasting panic in her throat. "When did he tell you?"

Muzi frowned as he reached past her to open a French door for her. He gestured her to precede him. "Uh…a while back? When he went on that bender, shortly after he discovered who you were."

Digby had taken a while to come to terms with the fact that his girlfriend's nanny was also his sister and the beneficiary of his estranged parents' large trust.

"You can't tell anybody!" Ro placed her hand on his bare, muscled forearm and tried to ignore the heat of his skin, the sparks of desire burning her. "God, why did he tell you?"

Frost touched Muzi's black eyes. "I have yet to break a friend's confidence and I never will."

It was obvious that her lack of trust in him annoyed him but she'd only met the man ten minutes ago! And if her boyfriend of eight years could betray her, she didn't put much faith in the goodness of strangers. Oh, Digby was going to get an earful from her for running his mouth. He had no right to divulge her secrets.

Ro was aware of the wary glances Muzi sent her as they made their way down the stone pathway that meandered through the extensive grounds of The Vane. A gentle breeze blew strands of her long hair into her face, and now and again she inhaled the scent of fynbos drifting down from the mountain,

combined with the sweet scent from the many rose-
bushes and Muzi's earthy, sexy cologne.

It was a potent combination and one designed to
make her head swim. Add a sexy, virile, hot-as-hell
man to the mix and she was a jumbled mess of desire, resentment, fear and confusion.

Really, being an heiress shouldn't be this hard.

Approaching the tables under the large oak trees,
Ro looked for her brothers and on seeing them,
headed in their direction. Radd and Digby stood up
as she and Muzi, carrying little Liv, threaded their
way through the tables. Like her, Radd and Digby
were tall, dark-haired and blue-eyed. When the three
of them were together, Ro couldn't help wondering
how people didn't notice that she was a feminine
version of her big, burly brothers.

Ro accepted their hugs—her brothers were super
affectionate—and Radd pulled out a chair for her
while Digby took a now sleeping Liv from Muzi's
strong arms. He looked down at his soon-to-be
daughter, his knuckle sliding over her cheek. Then
he looked at Muzi and grinned. "Did you make her
train for one of your triathlons? She is only three,
Triple M."

Triple M? On seeing her confusion, Digby smiled.
"Three M and Triple M are Muzi's nicknames from
school, since all his names begin with *M*."

Muzi, Miya, Matthews…right, that made sense.

"I take it you two introduced yourselves?" Digby
asked, sitting back down in a comfortable chair, Livvie curled up against his chest.

Muzi dropped into a seat and stretched out his long, long muscled legs. "We did. Although your sister is deeply unhappy that I know she is the Tempest-Vane heir."

Digby caught Ro's eye and winced. "Sorry, Ro, but Muzi, well…he kinda knows everything about me."

That's what Muzi said earlier. It didn't assuage her fears. "All it takes is one slip of the tongue and I will become a media sensation. I do *not* want to become a media sensation."

Digby winced again, looking apologetic. Muzi's face remained impassive and when her eyes hit her older brother's face, she saw sympathy in his dark blue eyes.

"Muzi can be trusted to keep your secret, Ro," Radd assured her. "I trust him, and you know how few people I trust."

Ro nodded, her tension lifting. Radd had massive trust issues and his reassurance of Muzi's integrity dampened some of her fears. She looked at the man in question and narrowed her eyes. "If you let my secret slip, I will disembowel you with a blunt teaspoon. Are we clear?"

Amusement touched his eyes and the corners of his lips lifted in an altogether too sexy smirk. "Perfectly."

"Excellent." Digby released a relieved sigh. He gestured to a waiter and asked Ro what she wanted to drink. She ordered a gin and tonic, the men ordered beers, and Ro dug in her tote bag for her pair of sunglasses. She shoved her glasses onto her face, noticing a scratch in the cheap glass.

Now that she had access to so much cash, she could buy a dozen—even a hundred—pairs of designer sunglasses, shoes, bags and clothes. Ro looked down at her off-the-rack blue-and-white sundress and shrugged. She wasn't a shopper, and never had been, so hitting the Platinum Mile of the Victoria & Alfred Waterfront, one of the city's upmarket malls, wasn't high on her list of priorities.

She wasn't sure what was.

Maybe it was time she figured that out.

So this was Roisin O'Keefe, the must-be-kept-secret Tempest-Vane sister.

Muzi slid a pair of designer sunglasses over his eyes and, taking a long sip of his beer—his mouth was suddenly as dry as the Namib Desert—eyed her, knowing his dark lenses would hide his scrutiny.

She was—*crap*—breath-stealingly beautiful.

Her hair was long, a fall of loose curls, and an intense shade of dark brown without a hint of red or gold. It was the perfect complement to her creamy, pale skin and her drop-him-to-the-floor blue eyes.

Blue, it was such an insipid description. They were the color of ancient Chinese vases or old-as-hell Egyptian artifacts. Of ancient tiles in mosques all over the Middle East.

Blue had always been his favorite color.

Pulling his gaze off her face, he allowed himself the immense pleasure of letting it trail down her long and lithe body. Her breasts were perfection, her stomach flat, her legs smooth and slightly tanned. And those pretty pale pink toenails, and the delicate ring on her middle digit, killed him.

Muzi did an internal eye roll at his body's reactions. He was thirty-four, had slept with many beautiful women, and it had been a long time since he'd had this sort of reaction to a woman, any woman.

But there was no denying it, she was as sexy as hell...

And solidly off-limits.

She was his best friend's sister. And, since she was now the owner of St. Urban, one the oldest vineyards in the Cape Winelands, Ro was also someone he wanted to do business with. No, he *needed* to do business with her...

He needed her vineyard to neutralize Susan Matthews-Reed.

As it always did when he thought of Susan, his gut roiled. She'd been, without exaggeration, the bane of his life for...well, most of his life.

He'd met Mimi Matthews when his poor, far too young mother sent him to live with his maternal grandmother, Lu, who'd worked as Mimi's long-time housekeeper at La Fontaine, Mimi's Cape Dutch house in the Franschhoek Valley, an hour's drive from Cape Town.

He'd been a fatherless three-year-old—he never knew who sired him—confused by his change of circumstances and missing his mother. He'd left a dirt-poor, rural village for one of the wealthiest areas in the country. But with his grandmother Lu he found stability and comfort. Lu and Mimi showered him with love and affection, and he'd blossomed under their attention.

A few months after his eighth birthday, Mimi's only child, Susan, divorced her husband and she and her two sons, Rafe and Keane, moved into La Fontaine. He'd been thoroughly excited to have boys his age in the house and he and Keane immediately bonded. Rafe, older than him, was cool but Susan... well, she was another story.

His grandmother died when he was ten and, along with feeling grief-stricken, he'd also been terrified, not knowing where he was going to live or who was going to look after him. After Lu's funeral, Mimi sat him down, told him his mother signed away all parental rights to him—as an adult, Muzi suspected money had changed hands—and informed him, and the family, that his place was with her. Mimi went on to adopt him and he became, in all the ways that counted, legal and otherwise, hers.

In the valley, he was regarded to be the luckiest child alive, plucked from poverty and obscurity to become part of a powerful, insanely wealthy and influential family steeped in the history and tradition of Cape wine making.

No one, not one soul, knew that Susan emotionally and verbally abused him whenever and wherever she found him alone.

You're not good enough...
You don't belong here...

You're unlovable...

Leaving for boarding school had been a relief and university, where he studied business and wine making, was the best time of his life. After graduating he joined Clos du Cadieux, Mimi's famous wine and spirits company, and Mimi made it clear that he was to be her successor. Susan once again went on the offensive to rid the company and the family of his presence. As a kid, he'd never understood her hatred of him but as an adult, he realized that he was a threat to her and her sons—or rather to their inheritance—and she wouldn't rest until she kicked him out of Clos du Cadieux and out of Mimi's life.

He was a great winemaker and an excellent CEO, but he didn't carry Matthews blood and that, to Susan, was all that mattered.

Muzi sighed, thinking that the past three years as Clos du Cadieux's CEO had been incredibly hard. Mimi's unexpected announcement of her retirement rattled the industry—she was the wine-making world's doyenne—and his appointment as CEO had made waves, people saying he was too young and inexperienced.

After much discussion, the Clos du Cadieux board approved his appointment, but they also elected Susan as the new chairman and her son Keane as a new board member. Susan immediately began making his life hell: openly questioning his decisions, undermining him to senior management and other board members and generally being a complete pain in the ass.

Her goal was to have complete control of her family's—Mimi's—assets, interests and influence, and he, "the grandson of Mimi's housekeeper, a nobody, for God's sake," stood in her way.

She was smart, ruthless and convincing. And persistent. Worst of all, she'd managed to turn Keane, technically his nephew but emotionally his brother, against him.

As the Tempest-Vane siblings talked, Muzi rubbed his chest, feeling like there was a knife lodged in his heart, reminding him that if you didn't let people in, they couldn't hurt you. And after putting up with Susan's mind games for thirty years, could he be blamed for thinking that being alone was safer? He'd earned the right to fear rejection and never again wanted to experience being emotionally abandoned. Muzi tightened his grip on his beer glass.

He couldn't go there, didn't want to wander down that mental vortex, so he returned his thoughts to business, to what he could control.

Last year the COVID crisis had hit their industry hard, and Susan was using the dip in company profits and turnover as a sword, telling the board that an older and more experienced CEO would've steered the company better through the crisis. Unfortunately, many of the board members were listening.

Muzi knew his ass was on the line.

But he had an idea of how to save it...

Muzi rolled his beer glass between his big hands, acknowledging that, if he wanted to, he could step down from Clos du Cadieux tomorrow and not look back. He had various business interests to keep him occupied and he wasn't short of cash. Actually, that was a huge understatement. When Radd and Digby had sold the innovative internet payment system they developed, and which he'd invested in, he'd become an instant billionaire, so he had enough money to last him several lifetimes.

But Clos du Cadieux was his passion—vineyards and wine the loves of his life. He adored Mimi and knew she was counting on him to continue her legacy of bringing fine wine to the marketplace. He loved the industry, loved his job, enjoyed the combination of science and art, agriculture and sophistication. Clos du Cadieux, the brands and the vineyards it owned, was his life and he refused to be ousted by a petty, insecure, spoiled snob with delusions of grandeur.

If he could add the old St. Urban winery—and assuming he found acres of C'Artegan, a rare, old-world vine on the property—to Clos du Cadieux's portfolio, and develop an exciting, new and stunning wine from those long-forgotten vines, his position within the company would be cemented. He'd be all but untouchable. He'd had his eye on the vineyard for years but Zia Tempest-Vane, who had inherited the vineyard from her mother, refused to sell the property. When she died it became part of the trust she and Gil left behind. With Ro inheriting their assets, he could finally reopen negotiations.

What should be a simple transaction—he was prepared to pay whatever he had to in order to acquire the two-hundred-year-old vineyard, its antiquated cellars and Dutch gable house—could become tricky. Because Ro was extraordinarily beautiful, and he was insanely attracted to her.

She was also his best friend's sister and not even Digby knew he needed her vineyard to cement his position at Clos du Cadieux...

It was all so damn complicated. He'd only ever admit this to himself, but he was terrified of anything that made him feel too much. Emotion and connection, and the losing thereof, led to heartache.

He'd had enough of that in his life, thank you very much.

"How did your meeting with the lawyers go today, Ro?" Radd asked his sister as Muzi pulled his attention back to their conversation.

Ro bit the inside of her lip, looking unsure. Muzi placed his hands on the arms of his chair and started to rise. "I can go if you guys want to have a private conversation."

Ro shook her head. "Since you already know my biggest secret, I don't have a problem with you hearing the details."

Muzi sat back down and Ro looked at Radd, then Digby, and wrinkled her very pretty nose.

"Siya Mabaso, my lawyer, arranged to have Gil and Zia's possessions moved to a warehouse in LA in preparation for the auction. Their house in Carmel has been sold. I've accepted offers for the apartment in New York, the house in the South of France, and the villa on St. Bart's."

Gil and Zia had shown the world how much wealth a couple could acquire when one drained a hundred-plus-year-old company of all its assets, Muzi thought.

"I've been in touch with the representative of Murphy International, and they are going to handle the auction of the art, cars and collectibles. I had a video call with her and she said that Carrick Murphy is personally going to oversee the auction. As I said, if you guys don't want any of their possessions—" Muzi knew that neither of the brothers wanted anything from their parents "—then the proceeds of the sale of the movables and the properties will be donated to the Tempest-Vane Foundation."

"Please don't feel obligated to do that, Ro," Radd quietly stated. "It's a generous offer but you are their heir, it's now your money and you can do whatever you want with it."

"I don't need money, I need answers." Ro stared down at her hands, delicate with long fingers and unvarnished nails. Muzi watched as confusion chased hurt across her face. "I wish I knew why they gave me up for adoption. I mean, it wasn't like they didn't have the money to feed and clothe me, educate me."

Muzi met Digby's eyes and saw the pain within him, the flash of temper and then, devastation. Muzi knew his anger and grief were no longer for him, but for his sister. Ro had no idea—and would never know, if her brothers had their way—that she was tossed aside, given away because she was of no monetary value to them.

Per Digby, a Tempest-Vane grandfather or great-grandfather, noticing that Gil Tempest-Vane was the only male left to carry the T-V name and genes, promised Gil two million dollars—a fortune back then—for every male child he sired. Zia cooperated and they produced three boys for the family tree, boys they went on to ignore and neglect.

But a girl didn't come with a monetary payout, so she was given up for adoption.

Bastards.

Radd and Digby were determined that Ro never learned the truth of why she was given up for adoption. Muzi knew they were trying to protect her, but he thought that if Ro found out after the fact, and from someone else, their brand-new, still fragile ties would fray. He thought the brothers were playing with fire, but this wasn't his family and, because he would never tolerate them shoving their noses into his business, he kept his opinion to himself.

Digby and Radd were just trying to protect Roisin—they were good brothers, good men—and he envied them their close relationship, their friendship. His relationship with the man he'd been raised with, the man he considered to be *his* brother was now, thanks to Susan, broken.

Ro's expression turned troubled. "Siya also told me that he's had quite a few requests from a reporter asking him to comment on rumors that the heir is in the country."

Radd frowned. "They are determined to learn the truth."

"I'm worried that you are not going to be able to hide your identity forever, Ro," Digby told her.

"I'm going to damn well try." Ro lifted her chin, charmingly defiant. "I just need a few more months to get a handle on the business of the trust and then I can return to the States."

Muzi's body tensed at her statement and he felt the urge to protest. What the hell was that about? Why was he reacting like this on hearing about her plans? He'd met her twenty minutes ago, dammit!

"What are you going to do with your South African–based properties?" Muzi asked, keeping his tone casual.

Ro frowned and looked at Radd, then Digby. "I own properties in South Africa?"

"Quite a few, actually," Radd replied, amused. "There's a mansion in Johannesburg, an apartment in Camps Bay and a vineyard, St. Urban, on the outskirts of Franschhoek. Didn't Siya tell you about them?"

Ro rubbed her forehead with the tips of her fingers. "I'm sure he did but I haven't taken it in. I simply told him to put everything on the market."

This was Muzi's opening and he was going to take it. "That's excellent news because I want to buy St. Urban."

CHAPTER TWO

IN DIGBY'S STUNNING converted barn situated right on the edge of The Vane's extensive grounds, Ro curled up into the corner of a plump couch, cradled a glass of red wine to her chest and stared out into the night, the same few thoughts tumbling around her tired brain.

Muzi Miya-Matthews wanted to buy her vineyard, a property she didn't know she owned until yesterday. She couldn't stop thinking about the big, bold, beautiful and built man.

Reporters were still trying to discover the identity of the Tempest-Vane heir.

She was camping out in her brother's house...

She wasn't in Kansas anymore.

Feeling overwhelmed, Ro sipped her wine, reluctantly admitting that she didn't know who she was anymore, what she wanted or how to get there. She wasn't naive enough to believe that, after she'd rid herself of Gil and Zia's properties and possessions, she could go back to living the subdued life of a kindergarten teacher. Even when all the legalities were wrapped up and she'd donated hundreds of millions to charity, bought herself a house, and put enough money away for any future kids' college education and her and her parents' retirement, she'd still be ridiculously, mind-blowingly wealthy.

And how would she explain that to the people she loved and the people who loved her? Her parents, Kelvin, her girlfriends and colleagues?

No, she didn't owe Kelvin any explanations anymore. She could, to an extent, hide her wealth from her friends and coworkers but she would have to explain her change of circumstances to her parents. She couldn't keep the secret from them forever.

But for now, she'd take her lawyer's advice to keep mum.

Loose lips, he'd said, caused problems, and her mother, God bless her, had no filter between her brain and mouth.

But Muzi Miya-Matthews, wholly unconnected to her, knew all about her…and Ro didn't know how to feel about that.

He also wanted to buy her vineyard. The vineyard she knew nothing about.

Ro jumped up and wandered over to the sleek dining table where she'd tossed piles of documents. Siya, her lawyer, had compiled a list of the properties she'd inherited, and Ro scrabbled through the files to find the document containing descriptions and photographs of the trust's assets.

She found the file on the floor, underneath a pile of bank statements. Walking back to the couch, she turned on the side lamp and flipped open the binder, appreciating the color-coded tabs: US Property Holdings, European Property Holdings, African Property Holdings. She flipped to the relevant spot, skimmed over the pictures of the mansion in Sandton, Johannesburg, the flat in Camps Bay, minimalist but with amazing views of the Atlantic seaboard, and finally, right at the end, she came across the description of the St. Urban vineyard.

It was, she read, situated at the foot of the towering Simonsberg Mountain. It was an "iconic, thatched-roof, whitewashed, historic gabled manor house" constructed in 1799, and now declared a house of historic interest. His brief notes continued... The property included one hundred and twenty-five acres planted with Merlot producing vines. Siya was also currently investigating the state of the house, vineyard and cellars to get an accurate market value.

Ro looked at the photograph of the house, dominated by an imposing, jagged-tooth mountain that looked to be situated just beyond its back door. The vines ran up toward the house and it looked picture-perfect, serene and comfortable. Rich and luxurious.

Why did Muzi want this property? From the little research she'd done since receiving his offer, she understood that, after been hard hit by the pandemic, the wine industry was still in a precarious position. Many vineyards were up for sale, production was down and the market was unstable. And Clos du Cadieux, as per an article she'd read, was cutting costs and streamlining their production.

So what was behind his desire to buy St. Urban? It didn't make sense, business or otherwise. What did Muzi know about St. Urban that she didn't?

Ro heard the beep of an incoming message on her phone, picked it up from the cushion beside her and glanced at the screen.

I messed up, I'm so, so sorry. Please don't throw away nearly eight years because I was an idiot.

Kelvin, again.

Ro rubbed the back of her neck and tasted betrayal in the back of her throat. He'd thrown them away, not her. She dropped back to rest against the arm of her couch and remembered their first date, first kiss and the first time they slept together. Despite her inexperience, she'd always felt completely comfortable with Kelvin.

The truth was that he'd never made her feel half as out of control as Muzi Miya-Matthews did yesterday. Muzi's warm eyes had her quivering and his voice, a deep, sexy baritone, set off fireworks on her skin. He'd only touched her to shake her hand, but his palm had been broad, his grip strong and his effect on her instantaneous. She'd wanted to slap her mouth against his sexy lips, curl her hand around his strong neck, shove her hand under his shirt to see whether he had a six- or eight-pack.

Bite one, or both, his big biceps...

She'd never had such a primal, visceral reaction to a man and, instead of daydreaming about him, she should be concentrating on her topsy-turvy life. She had decisions to make, a life plan to make, a path to construct. She had no plans to return for Thanksgiving but she should be thinking about flying back to the States for Christmas, only six weeks away, and how to broach the subject of her birth and inheritance with her parents. They thought she was taking time to travel before she married. She needed to tell them the truth, discuss their possible divorce and tell them she was never going to marry the man they considered to be a son.

But she wasn't ready to return to LA. Not quite yet.

Ro looked down at the picture of St. Urban and tapped her index finger on the page, still feeling rattled.

She could stay in Digby's house for as long as she wanted—he and Bay had bought a mansion in Constantia and were settling into their spacious, exquisite house—so there was no pressure on her to move. But, with the holiday season approaching, and the country's long summer holidays just around the corner, The Vane would be overrun with tourists.

Radd and Digby sat on the top rung of Cape Town society and constantly invited her to their A-list events, including the ballet, horse races and exclusive balls and cocktail parties. She refused all their entreaties, reminding her new family that Cape Town society would be insanely curious about their new friendship, and who she was, and where she came from. Mostly, they'd want to know why, and how, she came to be close to the famous Tempest-Vane's so quickly.

No, it was better for her to fly under the radar.

She was, she admitted to herself, so very tired. In the last six weeks, she'd gone from being Digby's employee to having siblings, had moved into Digby's fantastic converted barn, had fifty million meetings with her lawyers, discussed the auction to death and had an offer to buy one of her properties from a delicious man with secrets in his eyes.

She was overwhelmed and out of her depth and she needed a break, a time-out, a lot of peace and quiet, and space to think.

She might just find all of that at St. Urban. And while she was there, maybe she could figure out why Muzi Miya-Matthews wanted to buy her vineyard.

Muzi steered his brand-new Lamborghini Urus down the road leading to St. Urban and resisted the urge to place his hand on his heart to keep it inside his chest cavity.

He wasn't faint of heart. He routinely competed in extreme triathlons and had joined Digby on some of his more harebrained adventures—big wave surfing in Hawaii, hiking to the rim of the active Cerro Negro volcano and splashing around in Devil's Pool at the top of Victoria Falls, where a slippery rock was the only barrier between life and a one-hundred-meter plunge. But he was still recovering from an early morning call from Ro inviting him to accompany her to St. Urban and give her a tour of the property.

Would that, she'd politely asked, be something that might interest him?

His answer had been an immediate *hell yes!* On ending the call with Ro, he'd instructed his PA to reschedule a conference call with an international distributor and to postpone his other meetings, and he left Clos du Cadieux's headquarters to collect her from Digby's old house at the back of The Vane hotel.

"Have you been to St. Urban before?" Ro asked him, half turning in her seat to look at him.

"Once, a long time ago, but only to visit the vineyard. I've never been inside the house," Muzi told her. "It was part of a field trip I did in the second year of my enology and viticulture degree."

Ro winced. "Uh...in English please?"

He smiled. "Enology is the study of wine. Viticulture is the study of grape cultivation."

"As CEO, how much wine making do you do for your company?"

Muzi grimaced. "Not as much as I'd like to." Actually, that wasn't true, he hadn't done any R & D for the past eighteen months. They employed experienced vintners and most of his time was taken up with running the business and trying to outmaneuver Susan. "Making wine is the best part of the job, to be honest."

A faded sign with missing letters indicated the turnoff to St. Urban and Muzi drove onto the dirt road. Ro looked to the left and pointed to the rows and rows of vines. "Are those mine—I mean, the trust's?"

"I'd imagine so," Muzi replied, steering his limited edition, stupidly expensive SUV over a large hump in the road and trying not to think about scratches on his undercarriage.

"I think those are the Merlot vines," Muzi told her, as they approached a large electric gate. God, he hoped it opened—he didn't feel like climbing the gate in his five-hundred-dollar shoes and tailored, designer Italian suit to wrestle with its manual override. He'd do it, he just didn't *want* to.

Muzi parked in front of the gate and rested his wrist on the steering wheel. "Please tell me that you have a remote control for that gate?"

Ro dug in her large tote, pulled out a set of keys and lifted the remote to point it at the gate. Muzi held his breath and after what felt like the longest time, the gate opened with a series of creaks and groans. *Good deal*, Muzi thought.

He was about to drive on when Ro placed her hand on his thigh. "Hold on a sec… I need to ask you something."

Unless she removed her hand, he wouldn't be able to think of anything but moving her hand a few inches higher. Yep, around her his brain shut down and all he could think about was tasting her wide mouth, exploring her soft, pale skin.

Ro lifted her hand to brush her bangs out of her eyes and Muzi took a slow, deep breath.

She's off-limits, Triple M. Remember that.

"Why do you want this property?"

Muzi frowned, caught off guard. "Sorry?"

Ro's eyes narrowed to slits of deep blue. "You heard me. I looked online and there are many vineyards for sale in this area alone and the reason everyone is selling is because the wine industry is struggling to survive. Most vineyards are cutting back, not expanding so…why do you want this property?"

Muzi ran his hand over his head, silently cursing. He'd underestimated her. Ro was obviously smarter and more insightful than he'd given her credit for. He shouldn't be surprised. After all, her brothers were two of the smartest guys on the planet.

He needed to give her an explanation, one she could believe. If he found C'Artegan vines on this property, he'd be the one to bring wine made from a thought-to-be extinct old-world grape to the market. The Clos du Cadieux board would kiss his damn feet if he achieved that and his position in Mimi's company would be unassailable. He didn't want to lie but he was reluctant to tell her about his quest in case the news leaked and Susan found a way to spike his plans.

"You are obviously looking for an explanation I will buy," Ro told him, her voice frosty. "If you don't want to tell me then just say so."

Okay, then. "I don't want to tell you."

At his blunt statement, hurt flashed across her face. He watched, fascinated, as she sat up straight

and primly crossed her legs, staring straight ahead.
"Fine."

He was old enough to know that when a woman
said *fine* in that tone of voice, she was anything but.
Crap, how could he fix this?

Before he could say anything, Ro turned and
handed him a tight smile. "You are the only person, apart from my brothers and their partners, who
knows who I am, who knows about my changed circumstances. You know my biggest secret, something
my parents don't even know…but, sure, keep your
little secret about *my* property."

Dammit. She had him between the tips of a sword
and a spear.

Muzi stared out his window, seeing the weeds between the neglected vines. If he told her, and Susan
found out, he'd be risking his future Clos du Cadieux
plans. But, really, given the huge secret she was keeping about her identity, he doubted she'd let his secret slip.

But trust was hard, it was something that had to be
earned. And he made people work harder than most.
Sharing information was also difficult; he was a guy
who preferred to keep his own counsel. Talking always made him feel like he was standing on a mile-
high precipice waiting to fall to a stone slab below.

Ro released an annoyed huff. "Just drive, Muzi."

Instead of obeying her terse command, Muzi
jerked his head toward the overgrown vines. "How
much do you know about wine and grapes and cultivars?"

Ro half turned in her seat to face him, her expression puzzled. "I know grapes make wine. And that I own a wine farm and that I like wine," she replied. "So, basically, nothing."

He thought as much. "Right. A 'cultivar' is a grape variety that has been selectively cultivated to produce a certain type of wine. The vines beyond that fence produce Merlot."

Ro nodded, interest bubbling in her fabulous eyes.

"Bear with me because I need to give you a quick history lesson. In Languedoc in France, sometime in 1863, a farmer discovered that something was killing his vines. The blight and destruction spread through France and into other countries in Europe and they eventually discovered it was the phylloxera aphid causing the damage. Over fifteen years, the wine industry in Europe was decimated, and France was the hardest hit. Many old and rare cultivars were annihilated."

"That's very interesting but how does it relate to St. Urban?" Ro asked.

"I did my master's thesis on lost cultivars and I tracked down some documentation suggesting that one of your ancestors brought back a cultivar from France before the phylloxera outbreak. A cultivar that was supposedly wiped out in Europe. The cultivar is called C'Artegan."

"And you want to find this cat...cart...cultivar?"

He smiled at her mispronunciation of the word. "Yep. I'm sure St. Urban has C'Artegan vines."

"Surely someone would've discovered it by now?"

Ro asked, sounding doubtful. "I mean, can't you just walk the land and see whether there are different types of vines?"

"There are some obvious differences between cultivars, but there are only subtle differences between the Merlot and C'Artegan. Those differences all but disappear when the vines are diseased or have been neglected. Nobody from your family has farmed this land since the 1920s and it's very possible that information on the C'Artegan cultivar was lost and everybody has simply assumed that all the vines are Merlot."

Ro crossed a long slim leg. She wore a short-sleeve minidress in a deep green, covered with tiny flowers, a fun and flirty dress that didn't suit her oh-so-serious face. "And because of a hunch, and some vague documentation, you want to buy this property?"

There was still a lot of skepticism in her voice and Muzi didn't blame her, it sounded like—it *was*—a long shot.

Muzi put his car into gear and accelerated away. "I did a trip to France and researched the cultivar. There wasn't much information but I did find out that C'Artegan grapes produce a soft, intense, marvelous red. It doesn't have a great yield and the vines are as finicky as all hell to grow, which is why few farmers planted the vines. But, when you get it right, the wine is fantastic."

Muzi looked over the Merlot vines with a critical eye, thinking they weren't looking too bad. The vines had been leased to a neighbor for the past thirty years, but Gil and Zia's death had ended the agreement. It wouldn't take much effort to make them productive again and he'd had a connection in the dried fruit industry who'd buy any grapes Clos Du Cadieux didn't use.

And somewhere within the chaos were, he was convinced, C'Artegan vines.

"If they are so tricky to grow, why do you want them?" Ro asked as he took a turn to the right and caught a glimpse of a large gable peeking through the trees.

"Because I am one of the few winemakers who knows exactly how to handle the vines," Muzi said. "Clos du Cadieux has a couple of hectares of rare cultivars—not C'Artegan though—and the wine I've made from their harvests have not only commanded huge prices but also have won some international awards. If I can make a few cases of red from an old, supposedly eradicated cultivar, I'd cause a splash on the international wine scene and that would be very good publicity for Clos du Cadieux."

And he'd cement his position in the company and be able to shut Susan down for good. The board would never boot a CEO who brought a new, fantastic wine from a rare cultivar to the market. "So, that's the story of why I want to buy your vineyard. Are you going to sell it to me?"

Ro shrugged and smiled. "Can I at least see the property before you wrest it from my grubby hands?"

Muzi heard the note of amusement in her voice

and relaxed. She wasn't emotionally attached to the property and she had no reason to keep it. He had a good chance of acquiring the land...

He wished he had as good a chance of getting her into bed.

Best friend's sister. Someone you're doing business with. Keep your focus on what is important, dude.

"Do you know anything about the property?" Ro asked him, as the road turned away from the house and followed a small stream that ran through the farmland.

"A little," Muzi replied. "From the research I've done, the property has been passed down through the female side of your mother's family."

"Zia Tempest-Vane just carried me, my mother lives in Los Angeles," Ro told him, through gritted teeth.

So she wasn't a fan of her birth parents. Noted. "Zia's family came to this area in the late 1820s and they planted the vines they brought over from the Loire Valley in France. They grew wealthy and at some point built the house, the cellars and a second Cape Dutch gable house on the property. Zia inherited the property when she was quite young, in her early twenties, but from what I can gather, she was never interested in the property. I doubt she even visited St. Urban."

"I find myself admiring her more and more each passing day."

Muzi smiled at her sarcasm. "The house has been

closed up since your maternal great-grandmother's death and the land leased to winemakers in the area. That's pretty much all I know."

"It's a good start," Ro replied. "I know quite a bit about the Tempest-Vane history, but I know little about Zia's family."

"And you want to?" Muzi asked.

Ro lifted one feminine shoulder. "Yeah, I think I do, just to get a better handle on who they were and where I came from."

Muzi remembered the pile of bags he'd thrown into his car's trunk earlier. "So, are you planning to stay at St. Urban for a while?" he asked.

"I think so."

Muzi winced. "I don't know if that's a good idea. You don't know what state the house is in. Hell, I'm not sure if the utilities are connected."

Ro's eyes widened. "Seriously?"

"Did you not hear me when I said that the place has been locked up tight for decades?"

"Great," Ro muttered. "Well, if I can't stay here then I'll find a hotel in town."

Muzi wondered whether he should tell her that there was a popular music, arts and food festival in town this weekend and doubted she'd find a vacancy. He shrugged. If necessary, he'd drive her back to Cape Town. It was only an hour away, or, if she wanted to stay in the area, she could move into one of the many guest rooms at his vineyard on the other side of the valley.

Or into his bed…

Not helpful, Triple M.

Ro fiddled with the clasp of her bag as Muzi turned right to steer the Urus down another narrow, oak-lined road. He caught a flash of white and after another turn and fifty feet, the entire house came into view.

Ro released a surprised squeal and Muzi turned to look at her, expecting to see her dismayed expression. But Ro's eyes were soft with wonder, her generous mouth curved into a wide smile. He felt the power of her smile down to his toes and it took everything he had not to cover her mouth with his.

Damn, keeping his hands off his best friend's sister was going to be a hell of a task.

"I'm seeing a house falling apart so I'm not sure why you are smiling, Ro," he said, bringing the car to a smooth stop.

Ro pointed at the jagged-tooth mountain that loomed up behind the house, sunlight highlighting its many cracks and crevasses. Beyond the mountain, the sky was iris blue, a particularly African, intense shade of blue. It was a beautiful mountain, Muzi admitted, thinking that he was either super jaded, spoiled or ridiculously single-minded if he didn't notice the breathtaking scenery.

Possibly a combination of all three.

"I have to say, its setting is near perfect," Muzi said, resting his forearms on the steering wheel and peering up through the windshield. Two martial eagles were riding the thermal winds high above him

and he wished he had a pair of binoculars to get a
better look at the majestic birds.

"That's my house?"

Muzi turned his head to look at her profile, taking in her open mouth and wide eyes. Following her
gaze, he winced at the once grand, now obviously
neglected, house.

It wasn't an exaggeration to say that the house
looked a little dismal. The whitewashed walls were
gray and dingy, the thatch looked like it needed to
be replaced two decades ago, and the once green
shutters on the windows were warped and, in one
case, falling off.

"Um…well, that looks nothing like the picture
the lawyers showed me," Ro said, her voice faint.

Muzi tipped his head to the side. The house looked
like a grand old lady who'd fallen on hard times. He
looked at Ro. "Do you still want to go in?"

"I suppose I should," she replied, her expression
dubious.

Muzi nodded, left his SUV and walked around
the hood to open her door. He held out his hand to
help her out and electricity crackled between them.
His eyes met hers and he saw the sexual interest in
her gaze, the heat of desire turning her cheeks pink.
Man, it didn't help to know that she was as into him
as he was her. God, how the hell was he going to resist her? And he had to. They had business to conduct
and Digby would rip his head off if he treated her
as he did all his one-night stands and brief flings—

with kindness and respect but absolutely no promises, suggestions or hints for the possibility of more.

He didn't need a special person in his life, he was
stronger on his own. Because, as he'd learned, if
you kept people at a distance they couldn't hurt you.

Muzi dropped Ro's hand abruptly and ignored
her look of surprise. Sliding his sunglasses onto the
top of his head, he gestured for her to precede him
to the front door. The huge door, once the same dark
green shade of the windows, looked bent and buckled. Muzi suspected he'd need to use his shoulder to
budge it from its frame.

Ten minutes later, after much swearing, his shoulder aching from repeated contact with the old door,
they stood in the dank, dark hallway, dust tickling his
nose. He looked around, taking in the grimy walls.
His big feet hit a carpet and dust flew up his nose,
causing him to sneeze. Drop cloths covered various
pieces of furniture and Muzi doubted this room had
seen fresh air for the best part of forty years.

Whatever plans Ro had for the mansion, she was
going to need a hell of a lot of help.

CHAPTER THREE

RIGHT…WELL, THIS wasn't good.

Ro watched Muzi flick up an old light switch and nothing happened. There was a small chance that the light bulb was blown but it was more likely that the house had no electricity.

Completely fabulous. Using the flashlight on her phone to guide her through the shadows, Ro walked toward an open door leading off the hallway and into what she presumed had once been a smart reception room. The wooden floor was covered with dust and big furniture sat under falling-apart drop cloths. Pictures hung on the wall, covered in a thick layer of dust and grime, so much so that she was unable to make out the subjects of the paintings.

Ro slapped her hands on her hips and did a slow circle, her heart in her throat. It was becoming obvious she wouldn't be staying here tonight and, even if she had water and electricity, sleeping in a bed covered in forty years' worth of dust didn't appeal.

She should just sell the place to Muzi and be done with it. It was the simplest, most efficient solution.

He could deal with the dilapidated house and the overgrown vineyards. And if he found his elusive cultivar, good for him.

Hearing Muzi behind her, she turned and sent him a tremulous smile. "This isn't what I expected," she said.

Muzi folded his big arms across his chest. "It's a dump," he bluntly told her. He gingerly picked up one corner of a filthy cloth and lifted it to show her the corner of the ten-foot-long credenza pushed up against the far wall. He whistled. "But this, I think, is yellow wood and very old. I suspect that there might be a lot of valuable antique furniture in this place."

Ro walked over to the tall windows and lifted her hand to pull back the faded red velvet curtains. She hesitated. They looked like they might fall apart if she so much as breathed in their direction. But they needed light to see what they were doing, so she took a deep breath, pulled the curtain to the side and found herself smothered by a dust saturated pile of ancient fabric. She screamed and tried to push the fabric away and found herself more tightly entangled in musty velvet.

Sucking in a mouthful of dust, she coughed, desperate for fresh air. What she got was another hit of dirt and she coughed again.

Pinpricks of light danced behind her eyes. She was on the point of passing out when Muzi whipped the fabric off her and she could breathe again.

Ro sucked in a couple of gulps of fresh air and,

keeping her hands on her knees, looked up at Muzi. "Thanks."

"Are you okay?" he asked.

Was that a trace of amusement she heard in his voice? Squinting, she saw the quiver of his lips, the warmth in his eyes. "What's so funny?"

"You look like a walking, breathing dust mite," Muzi said, his laughter flowing over her. Oh, yeah, his smile could power the sun. And, beneath his short beard, she saw the hint of two sexy dimples. Dimples were her kryptonite...

"And you have spiderwebs in your hair," Muzi pointed out.

Spiders? *Aargh, no!* Freaking out, Ro lifted her hands to her head, bent over at the waist and fluffed up her hair, hoping to dispel the webs and, more important, their manufacturers.

"Do you think they're all gone?" Ro asked from behind her curtain of hair.

Ro felt his fingers in her hair, a long curl sliding through his hand. "Yep."

Ro tossed her hair back and met his eyes, dark, deep and oh so intense.

Later on, she asked herself who made the first move, him or her, but in the fraction of a second, his lips were on hers, his hand found her lower back and he pulled her into his big, strong, hard-everywhere body. Her hand curled around the back of his strong neck and his mouth tasted like peppermint and coffee. In his arms, she felt safe and secure, protected.

And yeah, his desire for her, long, thick and hard and pushing against her stomach, was hard to miss.

By their own volition, Ro's hands slid up and tugged his shirt from the band of his pants, then glided under the expensive cotton, and she sighed as they skimmed over his muscled back, the deep dip of his spine. He was so warm, heat poured off him and flowed into her, making her feel like she was walking into a welcoming fire.

His mouth plundered hers and she responded with as much passion, wondering where this need to inhale him, climb inside him, came from. Needing to be closer, she pressed her breasts firmly against his chest, felt the deep groan in his throat and silently rejoiced when he bent his knees to wrap his arm under her butt. He lifted her easily and it felt completely natural to wind her legs around his trim waist. Muzi carried her to the credenza and lowered her to sit on the sideboard, his hands on her thighs, encouraging her to keep her legs wrapped around his waist. Holding her on the edge of the piece of furniture, Ro whimpered when his erection brushed against the thin fabric of her panties, her dress riding up to the top of her thighs.

Muzi stepped back, creating just enough space for him to bracket her face with his strong hands. "You are so damn beautiful," he whispered against her lips.

How could he talk when so much electricity coursed between them, when the air around them, the dust and the dirt, seemed charged with energy?

She was without words, she was simply a big mess of need and want, punch-drunk with desire.

"Just kiss me, Triple M," she murmured, her thumb running down the cord in his neck.

She caught a glimpse of that sexy smirk, saw his head dip to obey her command but then he, without any warning, rapidly spun away from her to release a huge sneeze.

Then another.

Teetering on the edge of the credenza, terrified that she'd tumble off, Ro scooted backward and winced at the feel of dust and dirt against the back of her bare thighs. Thinking that it was more hygienic to jump down, she landed on her feet and…

Muzi sneezed again. And again.

He looked at her with streaming eyes. "I think I have a dust allergy," he croaked.

"I think you're right," Ro agreed, rubbing her hands on the skirt of her dress, wincing at the brown streaks on the fabric. Muzi didn't look much better—his cream shirt showed dusty marks and handprints from her hands running down his wide chest. The back of his shirt would be the same.

Cape Dutch mansion, one. Muzi and Ro? A big, fat zero.

Muzi took her hand and pulled her from the room. "We need fresh air and you need to get the electricity and water reconnected before you set foot in this house again. And when you do, I hope it's after you've had a tetanus shot and you're accompanied by a cleaning company armed with industrial-sized vacuum cleaners."

After crossing the hall, Ro pulled the front door closed behind her and sucked in the brisk fresh air outside. "That sounds like an excellent plan."

Looking down at her grubby hands, she grimaced. "Ugh."

"I have wet wipes in the car," Muzi told her. "Hang tight."

Within minutes he was back with a pack of wipes and two bottles of water. Ro thanked him, yanked out a couple of wipes and attacked her dusty hands. When they were clean, she wiped her face and neck and grimaced. "I'd kill for a shower," she murmured, "but I doubt any hotel in Franschhoek would accept me looking like this."

"You look fine but that's not your biggest problem," Muzi explained, wiping his hands. "There's a festival happening in town this weekend and I doubt there's a vacancy anywhere."

Ro stared at him, her spirits sinking. "You're kidding, right?" He shook his head and she muttered a curse beneath her breath. "Dammit. Then I suppose I'll have to wait until I get back to Cape Town to have a shower."

"There's another option..." Muzi told her. Her head flew up at his comment and her eyebrows lifted in a silent query.

"I own a vineyard across the valley, it's my weekend home." Muzi shrugged. "I have a flat in the city but, after a hectic week working in the corporate world, I come here to unwind and find some peace. Franschhoek is my hometown, where I grew up, and my grandmother Mimi lives across the valley." He grinned at her. "And my house has a shower, Dust Bunny. Quite a few of them, actually."

"I really should get a hotel room," Ro said, thinking that it was better to be sensible and put some distance between her and the tempting Triple M.

Muzi winced. "Yeah, that's not going to happen. This weekend is a mini replica of their huge Bastille Day festival and while it won't be as crazy as the big festival, the town is packed and I'm pretty sure you won't find a room. Look, I have a huge house that's sitting empty," Muzi added. "At the very least, you can shower there and if you want to go back to Cape Town, I'll drive you."

Muzi lifted his water bottle to his mouth and drained the liquid. She watched his Adam's apple bob up and down and noted the strength of his neck and his raised trapezius muscles. As she'd recently discovered, under his cream button-down shirt was a ladderlike stomach, defined pecs and acres of lovely, lovely skin. A part of Ro—the rebel in her—desperately wanted to go home with him and proceed directly to the nearest shower, *together*.

Wow, pull yourself together, O'Keefe!

She liked him, was ridiculously, stupendously attracted to him, but she'd met him just recently and she wasn't the type to fall into bed with men she'd just met. Oh, she knew she *could*, that woman did exactly that regularly—and more power to them—

but Ro wasn't that confident. Her body might be in the mood for some bed-based rock and roll, but mentally and emotionally, she wasn't ready to sleep with him. Or anyone. She wasn't in the right headspace to dive back into the dating pool again.

No, dating was out of the question because the word implied that she was looking for a relationship. She'd rather stab herself with a rusty fork. Relationships meant feelings, possibly even love, and she no longer understood what love was and whether it even existed.

Muzi surprised her by placing his big hand on her shoulder and gently squeezing.

"It's an offer of a shower, Ro, nothing more or less," Muzi told her, his expression understanding and a little tender. Or maybe that was her imagination working overtime.

Ro cursed the heat in her cheeks. "What about the…"

"Kiss we shared?" Muzi completed her sentence. "I'm attracted to you, that kiss should've clued you in, but you're Digby's sister."

She looked at him blankly, not understanding the connection. "So?"

"So Digby would kill me."

"I'm nearly thirty years old, and I fail to see what any of this has to do with him," Ro replied, a tad tartly. Why was she even arguing with him?

"Radd and Digby adore you and they take their recently acquired role as big brothers very seriously. It doesn't matter that I've known them for more than twenty years, if I mess with you, they will rip my head off."

She thought he should take his chances with her brothers and mess with her. It would be worth it. Ro cocked her head to the side. She knew she was playing with fire but, ridiculously, she no longer had a problem with being burned. Not if it meant flying so close to the sun with Muzi. "Would you like to mess with me?"

Muzi touched her cheek with the back of his knuckles. "There is nothing I'd like more but I think it's better to be sensible. One tends to have fewer regrets that way."

Sensible was good. Sensible was clever…

Sensible was also deeply, completely boring.

Muzi nodded to his vehicle. "Let's go get you clean, Dust Bunny." His megawatt smile flashed and her heart bounced off her rib cage and did a couple of flip-flops. "And if you're really lucky, I might even feed you tonight."

Ro sighed. It wasn't the type of lucky she was most interested in but she'd take it.

Unlike St. Urban, Muzi's house, set in acres of lush vines, looked fresh and lovely and was, as far as Ro could see, dust-free. On reaching his front door, she kicked off her dirty sandals and stepped into the hall, the wooden floor cool beneath her feet. Muzi tossed his keys onto an antique-looking table, exquisitely constructed and horrendously expensive, and placed his hand on her lower back and led her into a large sitting room. The breathtaking lounge—gunpowder gray accent walls and couches in navy and paisley—sported exceptionally high ceilings and an old, massive fireplace. Fantastic, museum-quality art decorated his walls.

Then Ro noticed the bifold doors across the room, opening up to a one-eighty-degree view of the Franschhoek mountains. Ro stared at the view for a good minute, maybe more, before turning to look at Muzi.

"That's one hell of a view, Triple M," she stated.

He smiled at her use of Digby's nickname. "It really is," Muzi replied.

"Is this building old?" Ro asked, her hand on the strap of the tote bag hanging off her shoulder.

"It was originally a mission house but the building burned down in the late '70s. Clos du Cadieux bought the property five years ago but the company didn't want, or need, any of the buildings or the fifty acres to the north. So I bought the building and the land," Muzi told her, gesturing for her to follow him. Ro crossed the room, passing the entrance to a gourmet kitchen featuring marble and top-of-the-range Italian appliances. Turning her head, she sighed at the wide, expansive outdoor entertainment area running the length of the house. A large pool, the same length of the deck, was on a tier below and bright blue water glistened in the midafternoon sun. Beyond the pool, she saw a glorious garden of white roses, swathes of lavender, mature indigenous trees and, of course, the stunning view of the mountains.

Muzi must have an excellent decorator, Ro mused

as she followed him down a wide hallway, peeking into rooms where she could. The decor was high-end, unfussy but, in the simple lines and muted shades, there were elements designed to charm. Brightly colored cushions, bespoke art pieces and handpicked fabrics.

Muzi opened a door and stepped back to allow her to enter a room on the right. A queen-size bed, covered with white linen and a pale green blanket on the foot of the bed, dominated the room. The bed was tucked into the corner of the room, next to a half-open French door that led to a private patio and garden. A small couch and tiny desk graced the opposite side of the room. Ro realized that, whether one was lying in bed, or curled up in the corner of the couch, the view of the garden and mountains was never impeded.

And, dear Lord, was that a Paul Cadden sketch on the opposite wall? No way! She stepped forward, convinced it was a print, and her breath caught when she saw the tiny lines by the hyperrealist artist. She placed a hand on her heart... Muzi owned a Paul Cadden sketch, who *was* this guy?

"The bathroom is through there," Muzi said, gesturing her to a wooden sliding door next to the couch. "There's a robe behind the door and use whatever toiletries you need. I'll go and get your bags and Greta, my housekeeper, can unpack if you need her to."

"No need," Ro hastily assured him. "I'm only staying for a night, maybe two. And only until I can book into a hotel in town."

Muzi leaned one shoulder into the wooden door frame. He stared at her, his expression now impassive. "So, are you going to sell St. Urban to me today?"

Beneath his offhand comment was a serious note, a hint of desperation she couldn't easily dismiss. "I could, I suppose."

"But that's not going to happen, is it?"

Ro shook her head. "Sensible me thinks that's a fine plan, but I feel like I want to go back, that I *need* to go back. The house is a mess, but I want to see more of it. I feel like..." Oh, this was going to sound oh-so-stupid. But she'd had a strange feeling from the moment she stepped foot into the house, and it had just increased in intensity since then.

Muzi tipped his head to the side, his expression encouraging her to finish her sentence. "I feel like the house has been waiting for me," Ro told him.

There, she'd said it, and Ro waited for scoffing laughter or a dismissive comment. She got neither and he just kept looking at her with those intense black eyes.

Man, she was still so tempted to step out of her dusty dress and to dirty that all-white bed linen with him. Ro rubbed a hand over her face and stared at the reclaimed wooden planks beneath her feet. She barely recognized who she was around Muzi. She felt like a walking, talking—babbling!—mess of hormones. With Kelvin, sex had been fun, mostly, but not something she thought about that often. They slept together once a week, sometimes twice and it was nice. Mundane. Satisfactory.

She'd never wanted to climb her ex-fiancé and gobble him up like she did Muzi. He made her feel alive, tuned in and turned on and...uncomfortable. Out of control. She had far too much to deal with, to work through. She did not need her inconvenient attraction to a hot, intelligent, sexy African man to complicate her life.

Too late, cupcake.

"Spend some time at the vineyard, but get the power and water connected at the house first. When you are ready to sell, can you give me the first option to buy?"

It took Ro a few seconds to pull her mind out of fantasyland and back onto the subject. She nodded. "Deal. I'll also get a contractor out there to give me a proper idea of what needs to be done, what state the house is really in. Obviously, nobody has visited the property for a long, long time," Ro continued.

"It boggles the mind."

"It sure does. Why didn't she just sell it instead of letting it deteriorate?" Ro demanded.

"Maybe your brothers can answer that question," Muzi said, "but I wouldn't hold your breath. Radd and Digby didn't have that much more contact with Gil and Zia than you did.

"People should have to take a test to procreate," he added.

"Amen to that," Ro replied. As a teacher who'd

encountered far too many less than wonderful parents, she'd campaign for that to happen.

Ro pushed a hand through her hair and dislodged a cloud of dust. Right, priorities, O'Keefe—and hers should be to get clean. While washing the dust off her body, maybe she could flush Muzi from her mind. It was worth a try, she thought.

"I'll meet you on the veranda in thirty minutes," Muzi told her, his intense eyes clashing with hers.

"Are you sure it's okay for me to stay? I don't want to intrude on your solitude or impose on you in any way."

Maybe she was hoping that he'd say that she was, that he'd take her back to Cape Town. Her mind knew they needed distance, emotional as well as physical. Still, she didn't want to be anywhere but here with him.

And that was dangerous.

Muzi took a step, then another to reach her and his knuckles skimmed up and down her bare arm. She sucked in a breath, felt her stomach contract, and that special space between her legs pulsed with want and need. So, that was new...

"If I didn't want you here, I would've driven back to the city. You can trust what I say, Ro."

She managed a small smile and it took all her willpower to step away instead of stepping into his arms. "Thank you." She gestured to the door leading to the en suite bathroom. "I'm going to shower."

Muzi walked away from her and she fought the urge to call him back, to offer him her body. What was it about this man who tempted her to step into his arms, what was with her need to get closer, to discover the secrets lurking in those black, black eyes? She'd better get a grip, Ro told herself, because there was no way she was walking down that road. It was littered with land mines. Her attraction to him was too intense, out of control. Maybe she was overreacting to him because Kelvin cheated on her and she was looking to get her sexual mojo back.

Whatever the reason, it was imperative to get her attraction to Muzi under control.

Ro walked into the bathroom, thinking that, had she been asked a year or two ago, she would never have imagined that she'd be single as she approached her thirties and that Kelvin would cheat on her.

She would've scoffed at the suggestion of her birth parents leaving her a king's ransom and she would've protested the idea of her parents divorcing.

Her life was far too complicated, and she wasn't good at complicated. Hell, on good days, she could barely handle perplexing. Complicated and convoluted were steps too far.

Take the first step, O'Keefe, focus on the next task in front of you.

And that happened to be getting clean. She'd been bathing on her own since she was a little girl, so she was sure she could manage the task.

It would, however, be *a lot* more fun with Muzi for company.

CHAPTER FOUR

HE LOVED THIS TOWN, Muzi thought later that day, as he placed a hand on Ro's back to direct her to turn right onto a side street of Franschhoek. Galleries and antiques shops filled the tree-lined streets, and vines brought over from France three hundred years ago cascaded down the slopes of the mountains overlooking the town. It was both quaint and sophisticated, laid-back and luxurious.

It was the heart of wine making in the country and the people, passionate about the land, the produce and wine, were warm and welcoming. Because Mimi was the town's most illustrious citizen, he'd been the object of speculation since the day Mimi adopted him. The great and good of Franschhoek were insanely nosy and would be extremely interested to hear that someone, a *female* someone, was staying with him and poking around St. Urban.

That wasn't accurate. Ro was currently *staying* in his house but, unfortunately, not in his bed.

That was where he most wanted her.

Their kiss rocked him to his core and, had he not

sneezed, God knows where they might have ended up. Rolling around naked on dust-covered drop cloths? He was embarrassed to admit that it was a distinct possibility.

Ro, like no other woman before, made him forget where he was, hell, *who* he was.

She was beautiful, her deep blue eyes a gorgeous contrast to that deep brown hair, but he wasn't a stranger to beautiful women and had slept with many of them. Nobody but Ro had made him lose his head, forget where he was, too wrapped up in her softness and her scent to care.

She was dangerous, she made him lose control and that was unacceptable.

And that was why, instead of them staying home tonight, he invited her to join him at a restaurant where he always had a standing reservation. Muzi knew that if they'd stayed home, they'd end up burning up the sheets.

And the bed.

And the whole damn house.

He'd feed her, ply her with some extraordinary wine and steer her to the guest bedroom while he locked himself in his master suite. He couldn't, now that he was so close, jeopardize losing his chance to have access to the St. Urban vines for a temporary affair. Digby was his best friend and there was a bro code... *Do not mess with your best friend's sister.*

He was not risking a lifelong friendship, losing one of the very few people he trusted for a roll in the hay.

If he was that desperate, he could scroll through his phone and arrange a hookup for when he returned to the city tomorrow evening.

Muzi released a long sigh, reluctantly accepting that he didn't want sex, he wanted to make love to Ro.

Make love? What was wrong with him? He sounded like a sappy character from a cheesy rom-com.

"This is such a lovely little town," Ro said, breaking the silence between them.

Muzi allowed himself the immense pleasure of looking at her. When she agreed to eat with him in town, she asked about the dress code and looked relieved when he told her that the restaurant was super casual. Her white jeans, gold lace-up sandals and a cute crop top, revealing a few inches of her board-flat stomach, were perfect for a casual dinner.

With her hair twisted into a messy knot, she looked amazing. Sexy. And far too beddable.

Needing to keep his hands off her, Muzi shoved them into the pockets of his gray chino shorts. The restaurant was just down the street and he needed a drink.

No, he needed a few drinks and another very cold shower. And to get his mind out of the bedroom. But as soon as he stopped thinking about Ro, his anxiety about his position at Clos Du Cadieux came roaring back.

If he found the C'Artegan vines, if he could get them to thrive and produce, he had a real shot at securing his position at the company. Hell, even if he only managed to secure the vines, getting them under Clos du Cadieux's control would be a coup. And he was the closest he'd ever been to that happening. He had a good chance of being able to buy St. Urban or, at the very least, he was at the head of the queue.

It was the most progress he'd made in years. Years ago, he'd asked to lease the vineyard from Zia at an above premium rate. But, because she was fully aware of his long friendship with her estranged son Digby, she chose to lease the land to a competitor.

The lease ran out shortly before their deaths and the vines were in a sorry state. When he got his hands on the vines, and he would—hopefully soon—God knew how long it would be until he could expect a decent harvest from the Merlot.

As for the C'Artegan cultivar, there was a chance that the vines had withered and died—the cultivar was finicky and frail—so his offer to buy the farm without inspecting the land was at best, reckless, at worst, completely stupid.

If he bought a farm planted with run-of-the-mill vines, the Clos du Cadieux board, with Susan leading the charge, would come after him with pitchforks and lighted torches. They'd also fire his ass. However, if he discovered a thought-to-be-extinct cultivar and managed to get a small run of wine, he would be considered a wine god and would be pretty much untouchable.

He was taking a hell of a risk, but he was fairly sure that St. Urban still had the C'Artegan cultivar.

Tomorrow he'd walk the land, and look for any subtle differences between the vines. If he found vines that looked interesting, he would send samples for analysis...

If they turned out to be the C'Artegan cultivar, he'd pamper and protect them, and in a few years, he'd produce a small vintage of soft, luscious, rare as hell wine. When he released a press release stating that Clos du Cadieux was branching into making C'Artegan wine, their stock would go through the roof.

But if Ro insisted on the sale going through before he had his results back, he would buy the farm himself—he was insanely wealthy and could afford whatever price she demanded—and decide what to do with the property later.

And his position at Clos du Cadieux would be secure...

"Tell me about Franschhoek," Ro said, adjusting the strap of the nude-colored purse on her bare shoulder.

He pulled himself back to the present.

"Before colonization the San and Khoekhoe peoples inhabited this area, but in 1687 Simon van der Stel and twenty-three pioneers arrived in the valley and established farms along the Berg River. A year later, French Huguenots, looking to escape persecution by the Catholic Church, came to the valley and started farming. The residents are very proud of their connection to France and they hold a massive Gallic festival here every year. They claim it's the food and

wine capital of South Africa and they aren't wrong,"
Muzi replied, stopping next to a small whitewashed
house. A discreet plaque on the gate told them they'd
arrived at Pasco's.

Ro glanced around, breathed deeply and smiled.
She looked at him, and attraction, hot and wild, siz-
zled. Muzi knew that if he made a move, covered
her mouth with his, she would be his for the taking.
She wanted him, that much was obvious, nearly as
much as he wanted her.

She wouldn't object to skipping dinner to return
to his house and get naked.

He was so very tempted.

"Are you guys going to spend the rest of the evening standing there or are you coming in?"

Muzi immediately recognized the gravelly voice
and turned toward the man standing off the path
leading up to the house, a glass of wine in his hand
and a cigarette dangling between two fingers. Muzi
grinned when Ro's fingernails dug into his skin on
his forearm.

"Uh...that's Pasco Kildare, the famous chef, one
of the youngest in the world to be awarded two Michelin stars. He owns a restaurant in Manhattan,
and you need to wait a hundred years to get in," Ro
whispered, sounding a little starstruck.

The last time he was in New York, about two
months ago, he called in on Pasco during lunch service and returned that night to work his way through
Pasco's new tasting menu. His food was always stunning, creative and cutting-edge.

Pas, he had to admit, could feed him anytime and anywhere.

Pasco's, Franschhoek, was more down-to-earth, casual and, because Pasco was Franschhoek born and raised, it was where Pasco could relax. The town still saw him as the younger son of one of the valley's most respected farmers and remembered him for being one of the biggest pranksters the town had ever seen.

It was hard to be taken too seriously when your biggest claim to fame wasn't the Michelin stars or your reputation as a superstar chef, but the fact that you plowed your first car through the floor-to-ceiling window of an exclusive art gallery on Main Street.

"Triple M," Pasco said, in his drawling voice.

"Hey, Pas," Muzi said, exchanging a one-armed hug with his old friend. He stood back and put a hand on Ro's back. "Meet Roisin O'Keefe."

"Call me Ro."

"Hello, Call Me Ro," Pasco said, dropping a kiss on her right cheek, then her left. Done with the Gallic kissing, he kept her hand in his and Muzi fought the urge to rip off his arm. Jealously wasn't his thing, but he'd give Pas ten seconds to drop her hand or else things might turn fractious.

Pasco dropped her hand at nine seconds. "Welcome to my place," Pasco said, sitting on the thick stone wall of the restaurant's old-fashioned wrap-around veranda.

"Shouldn't you be in the kitchen?" Muzi asked, not at all happy with the fact that Pasco couldn't keep his eyes off Ro. Pasco finally met his eyes and Muzi saw the mischief dancing in those green eyes. Damn. Pas knew that he was attracted to Ro and was prepared to give him a hard time about it. Muzi knew that if the shoe was on the other foot, he'd mess with Pasco in the same way.

Irritating each other, winding each other up, was what they'd been doing since they were spotty teenagers.

"My team has everything under control, and I'd much rather sit here and talk to a pretty woman."

He could find someone else to talk to and stay away from his woman…wait, what the hell? Ro wasn't *his*, he reminded himself, and he didn't believe in treating women as property. What the hell was happening to him?

"Stop flirting with her," Muzi told Pasco, speaking in Xhosa. Having been brought up on a farm, Pasco was nearly fluent in the language and, even if he wasn't, Muzi's scowl would tell him to back down. Way down.

"You're not the type to get jealous but she is lovely," Pas replied, his Xhosa accent a little rusty.

"It's business," Muzi replied, keeping his tone flat. He knew that Pasco wouldn't believe that whopper, but he had to try.

"Sure, it is," Pasco said with a wide grin.

"Why are you out here and not being a control freak in your kitchen?" Muzi asked him, reverting to English.

"I only flew in yesterday so I'm taking it easy tonight."

"You're welcome to join us," Ro politely told him.

"No, you're not," Muzi snapped. He saw Ro's eyes widen at his harsh retort and shrugged. She raised her eyebrows, looking for an explanation for his rudeness, but there was no way he could tell her that he wanted to be alone with her, to have her complete attention on him.

What a sap.

"Pas is a horrible bore, he just likes to talk about food and wine," Muzi said, wincing at his weak clarification.

Pasco rolled his eyes, picked up Ro's hand and dropped a kiss on her knuckles. "I'd love to join you and I might, *later.*"

Now the jackass was just messing with him. He'd pay, Muzi thought. Somehow, somewhere.

Pasco led them into the restaurant, which only consisted of twenty or so tables, with another ten on the patio outside. Pasco threaded his way through the tables, touching shoulders and trading quips as he passed his customers, Muzi and Ro trailing behind.

Pasco stopped a few feet short of the outside dining area and slapped his hand on his forehead, grimacing as he looked at Muzi. "Crap."

"Problem?" Muzi asked him.

Pasco looked embarrassed. "Sorry, I'm jet-lagged but that's not an excuse. I forgot to tell you that Keane is here."

It took all his effort to hide his annoyance, to keep his cool. He shrugged. "No biggie."

Pasco gave him a "Who are you kidding?" look. "I can juggle some tables and put you inside."

No, he wanted to sit in the balmy air and under the twinkling fairy lights and the man he'd once been closer to than anyone else, a man he'd considered his brother, would not chase him away. He hadn't done anything wrong, dammit, and refused to act as if he had.

"He's dining with his mother," Pasco added.

Oh, sweet baby Jesus. That was all he needed.

"It's fine, Pas," Muzi said through gritted teeth. It wasn't but he'd be damned if he'd let anyone see his annoyance or discomfort. Especially Susan.

Muzi reached for Ro's hand and when her fingers slid into his, his heart rate dropped, his shoulders and jaw loosened, and he was able to take a full breath. She steadied him, he realized, just being around her made him feel more relaxed.

Horny but relaxed. A curious combination. He glanced down at their linked hands, dark and pale, and shook his head, wondering why this woman had such an effect on him. He'd met her just a few days ago and here he was, holding her hand as he walked across the patio behind the country's most lauded chef.

Muzi saw Keane, the fairy lights making his deep auburn hair seem redder than normal, sitting at a four-seater table on the other side of the room. Keane looked up, caught his eye, started to smile and then, as if remembering that he was the enemy, frowned. They locked glances for twenty seconds and then Susan put her hand on his arm, tugging his attention away. Keane's face hardened as she whispered words in his ear and Muzi saw the distaste on his face when Keane looked his way again. Yep, Susan was doing another fine job of poisoning the well...

Pasco pulled out Ro's chair, got her settled, and when Pas looked at him, Muzi saw the sympathy on his face. Narrowing his eyes to make it clear to his friend not to say anything, Pasco gave him the smallest of nods.

Muzi knew that, when they were alone, Pasco would ask him, once again, whether he could talk to Keane on his behalf. Digby had made the same offer more than a dozen times but Muzi was adamant: he was a big boy and he didn't need his friends playing peacemaker or interceding on his behalf. He and Keane would work it out themselves.

Or they wouldn't.

It was between him and Keane. He refused to put his mates in the middle of a family argument.

Either way, he'd be fine. He always was. But Muzi couldn't help opening his fingers and looking at the fine scar on the palm of his hand. A lifetime ago, he and Keane watched a movie featuring friends who made a blood oath and, being ten and stupid, thought a blood oath was a cool idea. They'd sliced their hands open and shaken hands, feeling very cool and very grown-up.

The resulting infections, thanks to the rusty knife they used, hadn't been much fun...

But it turned out blood oaths and promises meant nothing, words even less.

Ro looked from Muzi to the table where the red-headed man was seated and she felt a tight band of tension between the two tables, an undeniable connection.

But nobody would realize that by looking at Muzi. He embodied the three Cs: cool, calm and collected. Until she looked into his eyes, turbulent with unspoken emotion. She immediately placed her hand on his, linking her fingers with his. She shouldn't be touching him but, under his implacable surface, she was sure he needed comfort, a little reassurance that she was on his side.

Not that he wanted, or needed her, to stand in his corner—the man was very able to take care of himself—but didn't everyone, at one point or another, need support? She sure did.

"Who are those people?" she asked, hoping but not expecting him to answer her.

Muzi tugged his hand away, pulled his linen serviette off the table and carefully laid it across his lap. "The older woman is Susan Matthews-Reed and she's, despite our age difference, legally my sister. The redheaded guy is her son Keane Matthews-Reed. I don't know who the younger woman is. Probably Keane's current girlfriend."

Muzi waited for the waitress to pour them a glass

of red—Ro noticed that Pasco didn't ask them for their preferences but just sent over what he thought they should be drinking—and leave before asking for clarification. "I'm confused. Can you explain that again?"

"My maternal grandmother was Mimi's house-keeper, and they were great friends. Lu died when I was ten and Mimi adopted me. Susan is her daughter and Keane is Susan's son, Mimi's grandson. I'm, legally, Mimi's son but I've always considered her to be my grandmother, not my mother," Muzi added.

Got it, Ro thought. "Where are your parents, your other grandparents, Mimi's husband?"

"Mimi's husband died young. As for my birth parents, I had an uninterested mother and have no idea who my father is."

Right. His "Don't go there" expression and flat voice suggested she not ask any more personal questions.

"Did you have a happy childhood?" Ro asked, trying to keep her question as casual as possible.

Muzi shrugged. "I had everything I could want, and I got a great education."

Good to know but he didn't answer her question as to whether he'd been happy. Ro was about to push for more when he spoke again. "I'm very close to Mimi. She's always treated me like her own."

Ro started to ask him another question, but he cut her off, asking her what she wanted to eat. Right, he didn't want to discuss his family or his place within it. She got the message.

She wanted to find what made this fascinating man tick, but he'd slammed that door shut. Maybe it was better that it stayed closed, she was already ridiculously attracted to Muzi, she didn't want to become completely fascinated by him.

At this point in her life, she needed a romantic relationship like she needed a hole in her head.

"A menu would be good," Ro said, looking around for a waitress.

Amusement returned to Muzi's eyes. "You won't get one. Pasco doesn't care what *you* want to eat, he's going to send us what he thinks we *should* eat."

Ro placed her chin in the palm of her hand and pulled a face. "Oh." She wrinkled her nose and leaned forward. "Look, I know I'm sitting in one of the best restaurants in the country but, damn, I want a hamburger."

Muzi's eyes lightened with amusement. "I can ask Pasco if he'll make you one. He'll probably curse, but he'll do it if I ask."

Ro raised her eyebrows. "Really? You're that close?"

Muzi grinned. "Hey, I fought off boarding school bullies for him, he can make me a damn burger. If he gave me a choice, not that he ever does, I'd just order a steak."

"Rare?"

"Is there any other way to eat steak?"

"According to my mother, the vegetarian, I'm going to hell for killing God's creatures and so is my father. He's, mostly, a vegetarian but occasionally takes a trip over to the dark side. Once or twice a year, or when he's annoyed with my mom, he brings out the barbecue and murders a steak, cooking it until it's the consistency of old leather."

Horror jumped into Muzi's eyes. "Tell your dad to stick to being a vegetarian."

"I have, on numerous occasions," Ro replied. She looked across the patio, saw that Susan was still looking their way, and tried to ignore the ripple of unease running up and down her spine. What was that all about? Why was she having a weird reaction to someone she didn't know and, probably, never would? Susan was part of Muzi's life, his business, not hers.

But if she and Muzi...

No, now she was being over-the-top fanciful. There would be no "she and Muzi," now or in the future. She was avoiding relationships. She didn't need the drama. She had enough trouble in her life already.

"So you and Pasco went to school together?" Ro asked him, running a finger up and down the stem of her wineglass.

"We—Digby, Pasco, Keane and I—all started at Duncan House at the same time. Most of us have been friends ever since."

Most of us? That had to mean that something catastrophic must've happened to his and Keane's relationship along the way. Seeing that Muzi didn't cross the restaurant to greet the man he was raised with, that much was obvious.

"Tell me what happened between you two..."

Muzi sighed as he leaned back in his chair. His body language told her that he was trying to retreat from the question or the subject and when he crossed his arms, she knew he was feeling defensive. There was no way that Muzi, proud and reticent, was going to open up to her.

And why should he? If he needed a sounding board, he could talk to Digby or Pasco…why would he want to confide in a woman he'd only known for a day or so?

Punching above your weight bracket, O'Keefe. Big-time.

She held up her hands, signaling to him that she was backing off. Muzi's shoulders immediately dropped and the tension in his face eased.

Muzi was not going to allow her to delve into his private business but maybe he could help her with hers. He was one of a handful of people who knew she was the Tempest-Vane heir, he'd known Digby for over twenty years and, best of all, he could give her an outsider's view, a nonpartisan view of her birth parents.

Digby and Radd were too close to the situation and the press were known to exaggerate. Her brothers called Gil and Zia materialistic and wild, extreme narcissists, children of Satan. Maybe Muzi could give her a more levelheaded assessment of the people whose DNA she carried.

"Did you ever meet my birth parents? Maybe when they came to visit Digby at school?"

Muzi looked thoughtful and took a while to answer her questions. "I think Gil and Zia only came to the school maybe once, possibly twice in the whole five years we were there."

"They didn't visit him?" Ro asked, appalled.

Muzi shook his head. "Digby was, as the third son, possibly the most neglected of the brothers. They didn't seem to care about him at all."

Ro rubbed the space between her eyes with her fingertips. "What lovely blood flows in my veins," she quipped, trying for sarcasm but failing.

She picked up her fork and drew patterns on the tablecloth. "Digby and Radd do not have anything nice to say about them, and I understand why, but they couldn't have been *all* bad. They must've had *some* redeeming qualities."

She heard the note of hope in her voice, the optimism and cursed herself. She wanted them to be better than what she heard, what she'd read, because who wanted to be the biological daughter of two monsters?

Muzi's eyes connected with hers and she saw the empathy within those dark depths. "Are you waiting for me to sing their praises?"

Ro shrugged. "Not sing their praises but… God, I just want someone to tell me they weren't completely irredeemable."

Muzi stayed silent and Ro scratched her head. "You can't tell me that, can you?"

Muzi topped up her wineglass as he slowly shook his head. "I wish I could but…no, I can't. They were completely, horribly, equally narcissistic."

Ro sighed. "Excellent news."

"Are you worried that you inherited their tendencies?"

Ro shrugged. "Wouldn't you be?"

Muzi placed his forearms on the table and leaned forward, his fleeting expression suggesting that he wished he could remove all her pain and frustration. "If it's any consolation, I choose to believe that nurture is a lot stronger than nature. Tell me about your parents."

Ro smiled. It was easy to tell him about the loving, outgoing, passionate people who had raised her. "They are great, very affectionate and a lot of fun," Ro told him. "They're a little hippy, a little dippy but very warm and very, very smart."

"What do they do?" Muzi asked, looking interested.

"My dad is a college professor, he teaches constitutional law, and a political consultant. My mom is a pediatric surgeon."

Muzi raised his eyebrows, impressed. "As you said, smart. How old were you when they told you that you were adopted?"

"My adoption was always openly discussed between us, so I don't remember them ever sitting me down and telling me I was adopted." Ro ran her finger up and down the side of her wineglass. "I had a very happy childhood and they loved me, they gave me a lot of time and attention."

"But?"

How was he able to discern the hesitation behind her words? He didn't know her but he seemed to be able to look beyond what she said to what she believed, how she felt. Despite being together for eight years, Kelvin never mastered the ability to recognize subtext, to look beyond her words to her emotions. Yet this big, imperturbable, muscled stranger could.

Honestly, it was both sexy and scary.

"But they were so wrapped up and so in tune with each other. So in love." She could tell him everything, she was sure he'd understand. "As a kid, I used to believe that my adoption was the reason I always felt on the outside of their relationship, that if I was biologically theirs, I wouldn't feel like that. And that's why the news of them wanting to divorce rocked my world," Ro added as she stared down at the table. She seldom cried, and never in public, so the burn in her eyes annoyed her.

Muzi's thumb stroked the inside of her wrist. She already felt warm and if she was this affected by him holding her wrist, she was sure to combust if she watched his broad hands stroke her naked body...

"When did they tell you that?"

"Around six months ago. The day after a lawyer contacted me and told me who my biological parents were and that I was the heir to the estate, I went around to tell them that I'd inherited money from my birth parents but before I could tell them my news, they hit me with their divorce."

"Did they know who your birth parents were?"

Ro shook her head. "According to the adoption agreement, Gil and Zia knew who my parents were but they insisted on keeping their identities a secret."

"And your folks were happy about that?"

"They'd been waiting for a child for years and

didn't care where I came from." Ro played with the charm bracelet on her right arm.

Muzi topped up his wineglass and sipped, looking deep in thought. "Hearing that you are insanely rich must've freaked your parents out," Muzi stated with a lazy grin. Ro couldn't return his smile. His smile slowly faded. "You haven't told them?" he demanded.

Ro shook her head. "Before I could, they told me they were divorcing and, I'm not proud to admit this, but I lost it. I told them to pull themselves together, that they were going through a midlife crisis. I was, *am*, still angry."

Muzi rubbed his jaw, his expression bemused. He lifted his hand to run his knuckle over her jaw. "Damn, but you've had a lot to deal with lately, haven't you? Hearing about the inheritance, meeting your brothers, your parents' divorce."

Yeah. And she had yet to tell him that her fiancé had cheated on her. She opened her mouth to dish that news but snapped it closed. She'd whined enough and didn't need to appear sadder and more messed up than she already was. She'd deal with her breakup, her parents' divorce and her unexpected windfall in her own way and in her own time.

"I'll be fine," she breezily assured him.

He nodded and squeezed her wrist again before pulling his hand away. "Oh, I know you will. You're strong, smart and sensible. And sexy."

Ro suddenly had a strong awareness of her heartbeat, could feel it pounding in her chest. The room faded and only Muzi remained, a small smile on his face, desire in his eyes. Ro, not one for elaborate gestures, tamped down on her urge to clear the table of its contents, to crawl across its surface to reach his mouth, to put her hands on that hot, lovely skin. She wanted him, completely, crazily...

Obsessively.

She swallowed, then swallowed again. She downed a glass of water that did nothing to assuage her parched throat and lifted her hand to her neck, then to her cheek.

Be careful, O'Keefe, you could be jumping from the frying pan into a very hot fire.

That wasn't something a smart, sensible, strong woman did.

"Sorry for interrupting..."

Ro jerked her eyes off Muzi to see the waitress standing next to their table, holding two slate gray plates. She slid a sizzling steak on a base of potatoes in front of Muzi. It looked divine and smelled even better. Ro felt her taste buds tingling but whether they prickled for the food or Muzi she couldn't be sure. Probably both.

The waitress then set her plate down in front of her. "Japanese Wagyu beef burger, wasabi mayonnaise and black truffles on a brioche bun."

Ro caught Muzi's eye and burst out laughing. "How did he know?" she asked him, astounded.

Muzi shrugged and smiled. "Who knows and do you really care?"

"Not even a little bit," Ro told him and dug into her food.

CHAPTER FIVE

THE NEXT DAY, Ro stood in the tall grass between two rows of overgrown vines on St. Urban and watched as Muzi gently parted the foliage, his focus on the trunks of the vines. She swatted away a fly and wished she'd put on more sunscreen. It was late afternoon, but the sun was still blisteringly hot. She'd finished her bottle of water thirty minutes ago and she was fairly certain some little African creature had climbed up the back of her shorts and was nibbling on her butt cheek.

She'd agreed to walk the St. Urban lands with Muzi before he left for Cape Town, but she hadn't expected to spend the best part of the afternoon stomping through the overgrown vineyard.

She wanted a swim, two liters of cold water and then a glass of Chardonnay, not necessarily in that order.

And a nap, since she hadn't slept much the night before. Not because she'd been burning up the sheets with Muzi but because she'd spent most of the night *imagining* burning up his sheets. There was, obviously, a vast difference between the two.

"The trunks are, mostly, in good shape. Fairly straight and mostly disease-free."

Muzi had been making odd, vine-related comments all afternoon and she'd lost track, and interest, an hour ago. Ro looked down at him. He was on his haunches peering under a vine, and she admired the muscles rippling under his white T-shirt, and the way his chino shorts pulled over the curve of his perfect, perfect butt.

He was built, sexy and as fit as hell. But she could easily resist sexy and good-looking—LA was filled with good-looking guys—but the addition of nice and smart was harder to ignore. Muzi was also a gentleman. He opened car doors, allowed her to walk into a room before him, stood up when she approached him. His old-fashioned manners were charming and instinctive, they weren't put on or forced, they seemed to be part of who he was.

But underneath the charm, she knew he could be as tough as old leather, ruthless if he needed to be. He was intelligent, cunning and very, very secretive.

He got her talking last night, chatting away about her parents and their divorce but she'd barely scratched his calm surface. She still had so many questions about his adoption by Mimi—strange that they were both adopted—but she still wanted to know more about his grandmother Lu and his childhood.

Ro slapped the back of her neck and looked at her

grimy hand. Why was she so fascinated by Muzi and why did her heart jump when she heard his voice, splutter when his deep, intense eyes met hers? Ro scowled at the overgrown grass, remembering that, not so long ago, she was deeply in love with a man with whom she expected to spend the rest of her life.

How could she move on so quickly? Was her attraction to Muzi simply a rebound fling? Was he a bridge to dating again, a way to get over her ex? Or could he be someone special?

Ro knew that she shouldn't be thinking of dating again, that wading back into the messy world of relationships was an unbelievably bad idea. Her judgment could no longer be trusted—she'd never, not once, believed that Kelvin would cheat on her—and she no longer had any idea what love was, what it looked like, how it acted.

Her life was complicated enough without her incredibly inconvenient attraction to a smart, sexy, secretive man.

Ro put her hands on her hips and arched her back, thinking that she needed to get out of her head. What she needed was a project, a distraction, something to keep her occupied. Ro looked toward the mansion, thinking that the neglected house and gardens might be the projects she needed to keep busy.

And her hands, thoughts and attention off Muzi.

But if she was going to stay in Franschhoek for the foreseeable future, she'd need to find a B and B, she couldn't stay in Muzi's house indefinitely. She wished she could move into her house but, while

Muzi inspected the cellars earlier, she had walked through the mansion and it was, genuinely, horrible. It was obviously a dumping ground for the Du Toit family's—she'd discovered Zia's maiden name from paging through a stack of ancient bills and letters left on the hallway table—unwanted furniture, books and detritus. The house was uninhabitable, so she'd have to find somewhere else to stay.

"I'm going to book into one of the local B and Bs tomorrow," Ro told Muzi.

She saw him tense and he dropped the vine in his hand, pushing to his feet. "Why?"

"Because I can't keep taking advantage of your hospitality," Ro primly replied.

"I'm leaving for the city shortly and I won't be back until the weekend, or maybe even the next weekend. My house will be empty so what's the problem with you staying there?" Muzi asked.

It would be super convenient, she admitted. "I could pay you a daily rate," Ro suggested, knowing he'd refuse but needing to make the offer.

"Not happening," Muzi said, his tone suggesting she not argue. "There's a Jeep in the garage that you can use, as well."

Now, that was too much. "Muzi, I can hire a car. Or even buy one."

He shrugged, looking unconcerned. "Use the Jeep, Ro."

He started to walk past her, and Ro put her hand on his arm, looking up at him. "Hey, a conversation doesn't just end because you deem it over."

Muzi looked at her hand, then moved his eyes to her face, specifically her mouth. She knew that he wanted to kiss her and wished he would. She hadn't stopped thinking about the hot-as-fire kiss they'd shared and she suspected, *hoped*, he hadn't either.

"What's there to discuss? You need a place to stay, and I have an empty house. You need a car, and there's one in the garage not being used. I don't need your money, so I won't accept payment," Muzi stated, sounding super reasonable. But she caught the "Why are we discussing this?" note in his voice. Yep, he was a little arrogant and very alpha, someone very used to getting his way.

But his self-confidence was deeply, stupidly attractive.

"So, any new thoughts about this property?" Muzi asked her, as they walked back toward the house.

Ro scowled at his back. "I know that you're trying to change the subject," she groused.

Muzi flashed his spectacular grin. "I am," he admitted. "Arguing with you is exhausting. St. Urban, Ro?"

"I think I am going to fix it up and sell it, I guess," Ro replied. The Franschhoek Valley was a beautiful area and the property had enormous potential, but Ro knew this property wasn't her forever place. She couldn't see herself living in the old, rambling house big enough for six families.

No, she far preferred Muzi's modern, light-filled house...

Stop it, Roisin!

"I'll buy it, at your asking price, right now."

Ro slammed on the brakes, her head whipping around to stare at him. "What?"

"You heard me," Muzi stated. "What price did the lawyers put on it? I'll even give you 10 percent more."

Ro felt her head swim, partly because of the heat, but mostly because Muzi was offering to pay her stupid money for this property. She opened her mouth to speak but no words came out.

"Why do you look so surprised? I told you that I wanted to buy it." Muzi placed his hand on her back and urged her forward.

She pointed to the house, just visible through the oak trees in the distance. "You're mad, Muzi! The house is a mess. I'm quite sure it's falling down."

"It's structurally sound, it just needs some work," Muzi said. "Besides, you know I want the land, not the house."

Ro slapped her hands on her hips. "Is that rare cultivar worth so much money?"

Muzi's expression hardened. "To me it is."

Ro watched as he picked a vine leaf and rubbed it between his fingers. He looked at her, his expression intense. And unyielding.

"So, what do you say? Do you want to save yourself the hassle of fixing up and clearing up the house and sell it to me?"

It would be an immediate and easy solution and an offer she should take. Although it had been in Zia's family for generations, she had no emotional connection to the place and she could save herself a lot of sweat and tears.

"Um...*no*."

Muzi looked as surprised as she felt. "You're refusing my very generous offer? Do you want more money?"

Really? That was where his mind went? "No, I don't want more money, you idiot. I'm just not sure I want to sell. Not yet, anyway."

"Why not?" Muzi asked her. "The place is overgrown, the house is a wreck, and I don't see you becoming a wine farmer anytime soon."

Well spotted.

Ro took a minute to hunt down the correct words. Muzi, thankfully, didn't hurry her along. "For the past few months, I've felt like I'm floating, that nothing seems quite real. I helped Digby and Bay by looking after Livvie but I haven't achieved anything this year. All I've done is meet with lawyers and read reports and go along with Siya's suggestions about how to go ahead with the dispersal of my birth parents' assets. It's all a bit, well…" She hesitated, looking for the right word.

"Unreal?"

Perfect. "Yeah, unreal. But also emotionally taxing. I feel like I need to throw myself into a project, something with a beginning and an end. I need to get my hands dirty and my muscles working. I need to work on something tangible."

St. Urban was that something.

She looked around at the overgrown vineyards, so

different from the picture-perfect rows of vines she'd seen on other properties, including Muzi's. Maybe they both could have what they wanted. "What if I leased you the land? And, as we discussed, I give you the first option to purchase it when I am ready to sell?"

In his eyes surprise mingled with relief. "Yeah, that could work."

Ro dragged her trainer through a tuft of grass. "Would a year be long enough for you to work out whether the cultivar is here?"

"More than," Muzi quickly replied.

Ro jammed her hands in the back pockets of her shorts. She could feel her nose burning and hoped she didn't peel. She needed to get out of the sun. "If you do discover the cultivar, we can include an option for you to extend the lease when the year term is up."

"That's incredibly generous of you, Ro. I do appreciate it," Muzi said, his voice deeper than usual. "But you should know that having a lease in place might be problematic if you want to sell the property."

"Not really," Ro replied, smiling. "If you find the cultivar, you'd want to buy the property, right?"

"Right."

"And if you don't, the lease is only for a year. I don't need to sell the property immediately. I could wait for a year. More if I had to."

Muzi stopped, turned to face her and put his hands

on her shoulders. "Thank you," he said, his voice tender. "You don't know how much this means to me."

This wasn't just business, Ro thought. His need to find the C'Artegan cultivar went deeper than business, than bringing a new wine to the market, than receiving awards and accolades. It was soul-deep important to Muzi and she wished he'd tell her why. She wanted, needed, to know him on a deeper level.

Good job on keeping your attraction surface-based, O'Keefe!

Muzi looked like he wanted to touch her, his mouth darting to her mouth and back to her eyes. He reached for the band of her shorts, his fingers sliding between the fabric and her skin, anchoring her in place. Ro had no intention of going anywhere.

The only place she wanted to be was in his arms.

"Is my magnanimous gesture enough to make you kiss me?" Ro asked, surprising herself with her boldness.

"You standing there, simply breathing is enough to make me want to kiss you, Roisin," Muzi told her, lowering his head.

Within half a second, maybe less, his mouth was on hers and she wondered how she had lived on planet Earth for so long without having been kissed by him.

He tasted of coffee and sun, of sex and sin. He tasted glorious...

Ro draped one arm around his strong neck and placed the other above his heart. He was hotter than she expected but solid, and she had the sensation that he'd be an impenetrable barrier between her and the world. She was strong and independent, but sometimes even strong and independent women wanted to feel protected.

Muzi cradled her face in his broad hands and his clever tongue slipped between her teeth. Her knees softened as her heart rate kicked up and, perfectly tuned to her responses, he placed a hand on her lower back and pulled her closer, into his long, thick and very hard erection.

The man was big...everywhere.

Muzi cupped one butt cheek and lifted her onto her toes, his mouth plundering hers. This wasn't a gentle kiss, a get-to-know-you kiss; it was wild, intense and a little feral. And every bit of her loved it. She couldn't get enough, she wanted more...

She wanted everything. Right here. And right now.

Ro returned his passionate kiss, moving her hands up and under his shirt as she tangled her tongue around his. She released a small moan when his hand found her breast, his thumb swiping over her nipple. She needed to get naked, to have him inside her.

She wanted to pull back, just long enough to tell him to make her his...

She had barely finished that thought when Muzi clasped her hands and pulled them off his body. He held them to her sides and rested his forehead on hers, breathing heavily.

"You are addictive, Roisin O'Keefe," Muzi muttered, before linking her fingers in his. After swiping his mouth across hers in a brief, hard kiss, he took her hand and they slowly walked back to the house, with Ro wishing he wasn't returning to Cape Town.

Despite having known him for such a short time, she was going to miss him.

They stepped onto the circular driveway in front of the house and Muzi nodded to his car. "Let me take you home, then I need to be on the road."

"Busy week ahead?" Ro asked as she settled into the passenger seat of his SUV.

Do not ask him to stay, Ro. Do. Not.

"Very," Muzi replied as he pulled away. "I'll get a lease drawn up for the land and I'll send it to Siya for him to make sure your interests are protected."

Ro wrinkled her nose at the mention of her lawyer. "I'm sure it will be fine."

Muzi looked horrified. "Jesus, Ro, you never sign anything until you've had a lawyer look over it."

Ro rolled her eyes. "It's a lease from *you*. If you stiff me, my brothers will bury you."

"They would, and rightly so." He frowned at her before returning his eyes to the road. "But don't sign a damn thing, not from me or anyone else without Siya's okay. Deal?"

"If I agree, will you stop nagging me?"

Muzi placed his hand on her thigh and squeezed, his fingers sending ribbons of heat through her body. She looked at his hand and wished...

Wished that he wasn't going back to the city, that he'd feed her a dozen, a hundred more kisses, strip her naked and do wicked, wonderful things to her.

She wanted to share late-night conversations and coffee, early morning whispers and drugging kisses.

She wanted him…

With an intensity that scared her.

Muzi's hand remained on her thigh as he drove back to his vineyard, and after a brief journey, he swung his fancy car down the tree-lined driveway and pulled up next to his front door. Muzi leaned across her and opened her door.

"You're not coming in?" Ro asked him, surprised. "You must be hot and thirsty. I am!"

"They have water in the city and it's a short drive," Muzi told her, leaning his forearm on the steering wheel.

"But—"

Muzi rubbed his hands over his face. "The last time we returned from St. Urban, I was as dusty and dirty and I *just* managed to stop myself from inviting you to join me in the shower. But if I get out of this car, I'm going to start kissing you and I'm not going to stop until we are both naked and you are screaming my name," he said, his voice a low growl.

She didn't have a problem with that, she really didn't.

"I see the way you look at me, the desire in your gorgeous blue eyes," Muzi said, his thumb gently swiping her bottom lip. "I want you, I'm pretty damn sure you want me too, and driving away is going to be the hardest thing I've done for a while."

"Then why are you?" Ro wanted to look around to check to see who was putting words in her mouth.

Because this wasn't her, sounding bold and fearless and more than a little wanton.

Muzi's thumb pressed into her bottom lip. "I could tell you that you're Digby's sister and we're doing business together and that it's not a good idea. It's all true." Muzi dropped his hand and lifted his huge shoulders. "But it's more than that. As you know, Digby talks to me. He's worried about you, so is Radd. They think you are more stressed than you realize—that you're feeling vulnerable and a little lost, that you are dealing with a lot. Maybe a temporary fling is *not* what you need."

Pride had her lifting her nose in the air. "Isn't that my decision to make?"

"Sure," Muzi replied, his tone easy. He leaned back in his seat and stared at her, his expression pensive.

She waited for him to speak, hoping he wasn't going to be stupid and try and make decisions for her.

"Your brothers are super protective of you, but I think you are stronger, more resilient than they give you credit for. And yeah, you're an adult who can make her own decisions. So why don't we do this? Why don't you take the time until I get back to relax, to read a book, to hang out by the pool? To sleep and to chill. If you want to pick this up when I come back, then it's game on. But I can't promise you anything, Ro."

She never, not for a minute, thought he could. Being more than a little stubborn, she wanted to argue with him, tell him that she knew what she was doing, that she knew her mind and was perfectly capable of deciding whether she wanted to sleep with someone or not. But...

But his words resonated with her. She had been stressed lately, she was tense and feeling overwhelmed. Maybe a little time spent on her own before they embarked on a no-strings fling would be a good thing. She nodded. "Okay, deal."

But, because she wanted to leave him with a taste of what he'd be missing out on, she leaned across the seat to drop a kiss on his mouth.

"Drive safely," she told him, turning back to open her door more widely. She dropped to the ground and slammed the door closed. She wasn't surprised when Muzi lowered the passenger window. She raised her eyebrows and waited for him to speak.

"Stay away from Pasco Kildare," he grumbled.

Ro grinned at him. "Not a chance," she informed him. "If the man offers to feed me, I'm going to eat."

"As long as feeding you is all he does. If he tries anything else, friend or not, I will annihilate him," Muzi muttered before lifting a hand and driving away.

She wasn't a fan of possessive men, didn't like them puffing up and beating their chests but, like everything else about Muzi, his jealousy turned her on.

Man, this hole she kept digging was just getting deeper and deeper.

Ro woke up to a message from Muzi, sent at around 6:00 a.m., informing her that he was back in Franschhoek, that he'd gone for a trail run, and that he'd see her later.

His return had been delayed and, after nearly two weeks, she was dying to see him.

Hopefully, he'd be back soon. Instead of pulling on an old T-shirt, her most battered pair of shorts and rain boots—her standard uniform these days—she tugged on a bikini, a short, flowy skirt and a loose, off-the-shoulder top. She swiped on mascara and lip gloss, sprayed perfume on her neck and wrists and allowed her long hair to fall down her back.

Shoving her feet into beaded flip-flops, she left Muzi's guest room.

She'd missed him, of course she had, and staying in his house without him felt strange but, she reluctantly admitted, she'd thoroughly enjoyed her time alone.

Working hard stopped her from overanalyzing and made time move quickly. The power and water to St. Urban were restored the day after Muzi left for the city and, since then, she'd worked eight- to ten-hour physically demanding days at the mansion, systematically clearing one room before moving on to the next. She now had a system—things to toss, things to keep, things to donate—and she was making slow but steady progress. She'd pulled down curtains, washed exquisite, vintage china, taken heavy and old paintings off walls and ripped up carpets. She'd boxed diaries, thrown away forty years of newspapers and found five cases of a very old, exceptionally fine whiskey.

She wasn't a whiskey drinker but Muzi and her brothers would, she was sure, appreciate a case each.

She was proud of her progress and an unexpected benefit of hard work was that her anxiety levels had plummeted. By the end of the day, she had just enough energy to eat the meals Muzi's housekeeper prepared for her, shower and fall into bed. Worrying and thinking required more energy than she currently possessed, and she was often asleep before nine o'clock, sleeping well until the next morning.

She was still ignoring Kelvin—not a day passed without him trying to connect with her—she spoke to Siya on an as-needed basis instead of constantly peppering him with questions about the trust and, instead of pressuring her parents to save their marriage, she was trying to give them some breathing room.

She didn't waste her time thinking about Gil and Zia.

She felt better, stronger, fitter...more in control.

Yep, Muzi—so damn smart—had been right when he said she needed to take a break.

Ro took her time walking through his house, stopping to admire a sculpture or the art on his walls. On her way to the kitchen, her attention was caught by the intense colors of an abstract painting to her left. She stopped at the open door to Muzi's study—normally kept closed—and moved her eyes to the painting on the wall opposite his desk.

It couldn't be...could it?

Because she'd spent a lot of time with the Murphy

International representative, the auction house selling Gil and Zia's art and collectibles, she immediately recognized the artist as Irma Stern. Gil and Zia owned three of her paintings, one of which she was keeping. She'd put the other two up for auction and each carried an auction estimate of more than twenty million dollars. Muzi's painting, bigger, bolder and better executed than any of the paintings in Gil and Zia's collection, had to be worth more.

How the hell did Muzi afford a painting by one of the country's best artists? Oh, she could understand the impressive house—he was the CEO of an international wine company—and he earned well, but she would've thought that a painting by such an amazing, important artist would be beyond his price bracket.

Ro turned around, saw another smaller painting on the wall next to the window and realized that it was a sketch by Degas, and on the desk was a sculpture by William Kentridge. Not in the same league as Degas and Irma Stern but ridiculously expensive all the same.

So, Muzi had pots of money as well as taste. She didn't give a fig about the money, but she did applaud his taste.

Ro walked out of his study and walked through the lounge toward the kitchen, sighing at the smell of fresh coffee and what she thought might be fresh croissants. She adored Muzi's housekeeper.

If she couldn't wake up with Muzi in her bed, then coffee and croissants were the next best way to start the day.

Ro added boiling water to the coffee carafe and placed it on the tray. The breakfast tray was bulging with goodies and she picked it up and carefully made her way out to the entertainment deck, choosing the small iron table instead of the outside dining table that seated eight.

It was shortly past nine, she'd slept later than usual, but it was Sunday and no one was waiting for her at St. Urban. A gentle breeze danced over the vineyards and the garden and it was already pleasantly hot. She thought she might lie in the sun after breakfast, and do a few lazy laps in the pool.

Unless Muzi had other plans for them…

She still wanted him, Ro decided, slathering her open croissant with butter. She wanted to know what being with him was like, whether reality could ever match her imagination. Ro stared out at the mountain dominating her view, remembering Muzi telling her that he couldn't promise her anything.

After being in such a long relationship, she was fine with that. She didn't know if she was ready for anything more than a bed-based friendship.

She'd always know where she stood with Muzi, he was stunningly honest, and she respected that. After Kelvin's duplicity, she'd rather be hurt with the truth than comforted by a lie. Honesty was a gift she never expected to receive.

She could have an affair with Muzi and when it was time for her to return home—sometime before Christmas—she could leave with a smile and some awesome memories. The thought of going back to the States made her mouth suddenly dry.

She didn't know if LA was where she wanted to be...

"Anyone home?"

Ro turned at the strange voice and watched as an extremely attractive, slim woman walked through Muzi's lounge and stepped onto his entertainment deck. She was followed by a younger man wearing an untucked button-down shirt and black chino shorts, trendy trainers on his feet.

She recognized them instantly, from Pasco's. Susan and Keegan? No, Keane.

She wiped her lips with a serviette and wondered why she hadn't heard them knock, or the sound of a doorbell. It was a big house but not *that* big and she knew that Greta, Muzi's live-in housekeeper, had left to attend a church service in town. Greta normally didn't work on a Sunday but she was on a mission to look after and feed the, in her eyes, too-thin American.

"The front door was open so we came on in," Susan said. She waved a thin hand, her superlong ruby-red nails flashing in the sunlight. "It's the country, we don't stand on ceremony here."

Ro thought she had a great deal of chutzpah to walk unannounced into Muzi's house but she wasn't a South African, maybe they did things differently here.

Ro gave mother and son a quick once-over. It was obvious the two were related. They both had deep red hair, the same green eyes and a long nose. Both wore expensive clothing: their watches and her jewelry could prop up the economy of a developing country.

Their clothing and demeanor screamed privilege, prestige and power. Ro wondered how they'd react if they heard that she could, probably, buy and sell them a hundred times over. The thought gave her courage so she slowly rose, pushed back her shoulders and lifted her chin.

"My name is Roisin O'Keefe, I'm a guest of Muzi's. He's not here, unfortunately," she said, not bothering to hold out her hand for them to shake. They'd probably ignore the gesture.

"Oh, we know," the older woman said. "Take a seat."

Ro, annoyed by her barked order, gripped the edge of the back of the chair. She was about to demand what they wanted when the younger man spoke. "I'm Keane Matthews-Reed, and this is my mother, Susan Matthews-Reed."

He, at least, was attempting to be courteous.

"Susan Matthews," Susan corrected, and Ro wondered if she imagined the flash of embarrassment in Keane's eyes at her imperious attitude.

"Okay," Ro said, "but I have no idea what you could want with me."

"For God's sake sit down and ask the housekeeper to bring us a champagne mimosa," Susan said. "I'm parched."

Keane frowned at his mother. "Not everyone has

champagne for breakfast, Mother. And you said that we weren't staying long enough for a drink."

Mother? Who called their mom "mother"?

Susan glared at him. "For God's sake, Keane, you know that I prefer to be called Susan."

Wow. Okay, then.

"I could offer you some coffee," Ro replied, hoping they wouldn't accept her polite gesture.

"We've just had some, thank you," Keane said. He sat down and rested his hands over his flat stomach, his green eyes cool. "Susan, you said you had something to discuss with Roisin, so can you get on with it so that I can get home?"

Susan crossed one long, still slim leg over the other and twisted an enormous diamond ring on her middle finger. That was, if it was real, a hell of a rock. And, judging by her Chanel bag, Louboutin heels and Prada sunglasses, it had to be real.

"I want to know how you are connected to St. Urban and why Muzi recently rented the property's vines," Susan demanded.

Ro stared at her, feeling blindsided. She definitely didn't have enough coffee in her system to deal with Susan. "Uh…"

Keane sat up straighter and glared at his mother. "For God's sake, Susan, you told me we were coming here to welcome her to the valley. And what the hell are you talking about?"

"Muzi signed a lease this week on behalf of Clos du Cadieux to rent over one hundred acres of Merlot vines from St. Urban," Susan told him, her eyes not leaving Ro's face. "I've been trying to speak to him, meet with him, all week but he's been ducking my calls and avoiding me."

Honestly, Ro couldn't blame Muzi; she would do the same thing in his position. "Why on earth would you think that Ms. O'Keefe knows anything about Clos du Cadieux business?" Keane asked, sounding genuinely confused.

"She's been spending a lot of time at the property," Susan replied, her tone defiant. Her eyes connected with Ro's and her ultrathin eyebrows lifted. "Why?"

Ro rested her arms on the back of the chair and held Susan's hard glare. She'd worked at a private, exclusive kindergarten in Trousdale, one of the most expensive neighborhoods in LA, and faced down many an entitled helicopter mommy. Compared to those lionesses, Susan was a toothless tiger.

"I fail to see how anything I do concerns you," Ro told her, her voice dropping below freezing point.

"I am a board member of Clos du Cadieux. I have a right to ask what the CEO is doing here, and why he's here with you," Susan retorted.

"For God's sake, Mom," Keane groaned, obviously embarrassed.

"Why did he accompany you to St. Urban? What is your connection to the trust that owns the property? What are you hiding?"

Keane rolled his eyes and sent Ro an apologetic look, his shoulders lifting in a small "What can I do?" shrug. *Telling her to shut up would be a good start*, Ro silently told him.

"And why do you look familiar?"

Ro returned her gaze to Susan, her mind racing. If this nosy-as-hell woman got wind of who she was, Ro did not doubt *that* bombshell would reach Cape Town by nightfall and she'd be tomorrow morning's headline.

She needed to nip this in the bud, right now. "I thoroughly object to you rocking up here with your impertinent questions but I suspect you won't leave until I answer. I met Muzi through Digby Tempest-Vane when I was working as an au pair for his fiancée's niece." All true. It was best, she'd read somewhere, to stick to the truth when one was lying. Now she needed to fudge a little. "Digby heard that the lawyer looking after his parents' trust—"

"Digby and Radd aren't inheriting a cent from that trust so why are they talking to the lawyer?" Susan demanded in a sharp voice.

Right, well, Susan was well-informed and wasn't a fool. It took all of Ro's acting skills to shrug her shoulders and look puzzled. "I have no idea and it's not a subject I have discussed with him. I know how to mind my own business."

Her pointed comment didn't resonate with Susan, but Keane dropped his eyes and looked away. It was obvious he hadn't inherited his mom's rhinoceros-thick hide.

"The trust's lawyers were looking for someone to

oversee the cleanup of St. Urban so that the owner could sell, if he wanted to—"

"How do you know the owner is a he?"

Lord give me strength.

Ro lifted her hands. "I don't—"

"Mother!"

Susan ignored Keane and gestured for Ro to continue. *Yes, Your Majesty.*

"The lawyer offered me the job, I accepted and Muzi offered me a place to stay," Ro said, thinking that she needed to end this conversation and get them out of Muzi's house. "The lease, if there is one, would be between Muzi and the trust."

"Muzi is the CEO of an enormous wine empire, he doesn't accompany girls to farms," Susan sneered. "I don't believe you, tell me the truth."

Keane slapped his knees and stood up. He gripped his mother's arm to get her to stand up. Susan slapped his hand away and oh so deliberately leaned back in her chair, her posture telling them both that she had no intention of going anywhere.

Marvelous.

"Why don't I believe anything you are telling me?" Susan demanded. When Ro didn't answer her, she stood up. She placed her fists on her skinny hips and her surgically enhanced chest rose and fell with obvious indignation. "I demand to know what Muzi is up to, what you are doing at St. Urban and why you are staying in Muzi's house."

Right, she was done with white lies, she needed one with pink and purple stripes and golden dots.

There was only one other explanation she could give—one Susan would believe.

"Not that it is any of your business, but Muzi and I are having an affair. We have been since we met."

Keane's expression hinted at amusement, but Susan looked at her, mouth agape. She opened her mouth to speak, shut it again and shook her head. "Nope, not buying it."

"Right, we're done," Keane said, his face hard. "Mother, you've embarrassed yourself, and me, enough for one day. I'm leaving and if you are not in the car in five minutes, you'll have a long walk back to the city."

Susan obviously saw something in Keane's expression that convinced her he was being heart-attack serious. She glared at him but picked her bag off the coffee table and pulled it over her bony shoulder. She tossed her head and sent Ro another glare. "Tell Muzi that this isn't over, that I will find out what he's up to."

"Tell him yourself," Ro coldly suggested.

Susan released an annoyed huff, whipped around and strode into the house and out of sight.

Keane rubbed the back of his neck. "Sorry about this, she can be a bit irrational about Muzi."

He looked embarrassed, Ro thought, but also sad. Taking a chance, she tossed out a question, wondering if he would answer it. "Muzi and Susan obviously have a tense relationship—"

"That's a massive understatement."

"So what's your excuse for treating him like crap?" Ro demanded.

Remorse and humiliation flashed through his eyes, across his face, before Keane's expression settled into impassivity. "I'm sorry we intruded."

Ro shook her head as he walked away and a few minutes later, she heard a powerful car start up and drive away.

Well, that was fun, she thought, dropping to sit on the edge of the chair. Seeing her phone on the coffee table, she picked it up and wondered how to tell Muzi that their relationship had shifted.

Had a very unexpected visit from Susan and Keane Matthews-Reed. The story is that I am at St. Urban, employed by the trust's lawyers, to fix up the place to get it ready to sell.

She sent the message and stared down at the screen, thinking how to frame her next piece of news. *Just keep it simple, stupid.*

She didn't believe me, said I looked very familiar—!!!— and kept pushing. So I told them we're having a red-hot affair.

CHAPTER SIX

We're having a red-hot affair.

HE WISHED.

On seeing the message on his phone from Ro, Muzi cut short his twelve-mile trail run and headed down the mountain, skipping over a tree root in the middle of the narrow path. Annoyance skittered up and down his sweaty spine. God, Susan had a tungsten set of balls. How dare she stroll into his house and ambush Ro?

Muzi used the back of his forearm to wipe perspiration out of his eyes and, despite knowing it was dangerous to go too fast on the rock-and-root-filled path—if he fell, he could tumble down a steep hill and, possibly, into the ravine below—pushed himself to speed up.

Bloody Susan.

Most people would think that him accompanying Ro to St. Urban was a perfectly reasonable thing to do, and it was, but Susan always suspected everyone of having ulterior motives. Pity that, in this case, she was right. He expected her to do a little digging into who Ro was, that was just the nature of the beast, but he never, ever expected her to rock up at his home demanding answers.

What raised her suspicions? She knew about him leasing St. Urban's land but Ro's wasn't the first land he'd leased, nor would it be the last. It was the fact that they didn't *need* more land and grapes right now that had obviously raised her suspicions.

He'd made a mistake of avoiding her lately and he cursed himself. If Susan heard he was on the trail of a new cultivar, she'd do whatever she could to derail his efforts. Hurting and hobbling him was more important than Clos du Cadieux.

Muzi, his lungs straining and his muscles screaming, bolted down the path. If the cultivar wasn't growing at St. Urban, or if the vines produced terrible grapes and dismal wine, his reputation would take a hell of a hit, exactly what Susan wanted.

There was no way he'd allow that to happen, he hadn't endured so much to let her win. Muzi, his legs burning and his arms pumping, ducked under a low hanging branch and cursed when a broken stick slashed the skin above his eyebrow.

He swore again, this time in Xhosa, touched the wound and felt blood trickling over his fingertips. Bloody Susan, this was her fault. He took his eyes off the path, looked down at the bright red blood on his fingers, not noticing the tree root beneath his trainer. His foot hooked it and he found himself flying. He went down hard, his shoulder connecting with a rock, sending waves of searing pain up and down his arm. Sprawled on the path, his face in the dirt, he took stock. Shoulder dislocated but no arms or legs broken. A cut on his forehead, scrapes to his face and he'd lacerated his shin.

He'd live. But, damn, he hurt.

Using his good arm, Muzi pushed himself up to a seated position and grimaced at the blood pouring down his leg. He looked around and realized that he was only a few miles from his house. He would call Ro and she could meet him at the bottom of the hill. She could drive him into town and his favorite doc could reset his shoulder.

First item on the agenda, calling Ro. Except that his phone was strapped to his good arm and he couldn't use his useless arm to pull it from its pouch. It took him a few minutes to remember that he could use voice activation...

"Siri, call Ro."

He watched but it didn't light up and he looked at the phone again, cursing when he saw the massive crack across the screen. His phone, thanks to the impact with the rock, was dead.

Muzi cursed yet again, long, low and slow this time. When he was done, he pushed himself to his feet and fought a wave of dizziness. He breathed deeply and, when his light-headedness receded, he started to walk home, dripping blood and swearing up a storm, trying to convince himself that, because he routinely completed ultratriathlons, four or so miles was a piece of cake.

* * *

With a dislocated shoulder, four miles on an uneven trail turned out to be the seventeenth level of hell.

It took Muzi much longer than he thought, mostly because he was a little light-headed—he must've hit his head harder than he thought—and he was tired, dirty and goddamn hurting when he walked up the steps leading to his outside entertainment area. Each step sent pain ricocheting through his shoulder, but a flash of bright pink momentarily distracted him.

He stopped, one foot on the step above, and his pain receded at the sight of Ro lying in the sun. Her long body was turning pink and a wide-brimmed straw hat covered her face. Judging by the way her chest and fabulous breasts rose and fell—covered in only two brief triangles—she was soundly asleep.

He could spend hours, days watching her sleep, fascinated by her long, slim legs, her flat stomach, the delicate curve of her hips. But, because he felt like someone was ripping off his arm, he could only give her another twenty seconds before calling her name.

He called once, twice, and when she didn't wake, bellowed her name. Ro shot up, her hat went flying and her head whipped around frantically, trying to find the source of the noise. She didn't think to look behind her and Muzi called her name again.

Ro turned her torso, placed her hand to her face to keep the sun out of her eyes and sent him a smile. "Hi, you're back. Did you get my message… Holy hell, what happened to you?"

Exhausted, Muzi slowly lowered himself to sit on the top step. He watched Ro run across the lawn and, a few seconds later, she stood in front of him, her mouth agape.

His eyes were in line with her belly button and she had a tiny ring in it, classy and stupendously sexy. He allowed his eyes to skim over her brief bikini bottoms, down her long legs and noticed that she wore a silver toe ring and had a small rosebud tattooed on the inside of her ankle. How had he missed that?

"Do you have any other tattoos?" he asked, before lifting his hand. "No, don't tell me, I want to discover them myself."

"You're hurt! Oh, my God, you're *bleeding*!"

Yeah, he knew that. Muzi squinted up at her. "So, we're having a red-hot affair? Cool."

Ro ignored his comment and dropped to her haunches in front of him, looking at the cut on his leg. "This needs stitches."

He figured.

She peered into his eyes, looking far too serious. "Did you hit your head, are you concussed?"

Muzi rocked his hand from side to side. "Maybe."

"Probably," Ro stated, standing up and holding out her hands. "Let's get you up and get you to a doctor."

Muzi looked at her hands and shook his head. "Nuh-uh."

Ro narrowed her eyes at him. "Look, Superman, you need, at the very least, an EMT. That cut needs stitches and while I have been known to apply a butterfly clip or two, this is beyond my area of expertise.

I also want to make sure you don't have a concussion, so get up off your ass."

"Can't…" Muzi said, focusing on her pretty blue eyes. "My shoulder is dislocated."

Her mouth dropped open in shock as her eyes fixed on his right shoulder. He'd seen a dislocated shoulder before, knew it looked weird. Because he'd been running shirtless, she'd be able to see the strange bump and sloped shoulder.

Ro pursed her lips and slapped her hands on her hips. "Right," she said, not giving him time to respond. "I'm going to call an ambulance."

Muzi gripped her wrist in his good hand. "I just need you to drive me to Sam."

Ro bent down to thread both her arms through his good arm. "Use your legs to push up and who is Sam?"

Muzi swallowed a yelp of pain as he rose and scrunched his eyes together, sucking in some deep breaths. Ro kept her hands wrapped around his bicep and led him into the house. "Do not brush your leg against any furniture."

He glared at her; he was hurt, not idiotic. He managed to avoid the furniture, kept his bloody shoes off the carpets and walked through the door leading from the kitchen to the garage where he'd parked his Lamborghini before starting on his run. "Are you comfortable driving a stick shift, Ro?"

She pulled a face. "It won't be pretty, but I'll manage." She opened the passenger door for him. "You didn't answer my question, who is Sam?"

"One of my favorite women, ever," Muzi replied as he pulled himself up into the car's high seat using his good hand. Ro stood on the running board and pulled the seat belt down and across his chest. Her breast pushed into his chest, her hair tickled his chin and neck, and her bare hip connected with his thigh.

And, because his junk had a mind of its own, and didn't care that his shoulder was a lava bed of pain, he felt himself swelling, growing. Any minute now and she would realize it too.

Ro clicked in his seat belt, tensed and turned her head to look at him. One arched eyebrow raised. "Really? Now?"

He lifted his uninjured shoulder in a brief shrug. "You're wearing next to nothing and all I can see is a lot of smooth, feminine flesh. Your scent, a combination of sunblock and perfume is intoxicating and your mouth, and nipples, are in easy reach of my mouth. What do you expect me to do?"

"Act like an adult and not a randy boy," Ro snapped back.

Easier said than done, Muzi decided. He looked down at his arm and saw his cell phone pouch. The edges of the pouch were digging into his skin and he asked Ro to take it off. She pulled apart the Velcro and, when it was off, looked down at the cracked screen. "Well done, Triple M, you've just managed to destroy the very latest, most expensive smartphone on the market."

On the list of his regrets, it was near the bottom. Ro tossed his phone onto the back seat and hopped down from the running board. "Let's get going," she suggested, standing back to close his door.

"Wait!" Muzi stated, holding up his good hand.

Ro pushed back her hair, irritated. "What now?"

"As much as I love what you are wearing, maybe it would be better for you not to ride into town dressed in a skimpy bikini." Despite his pain, he had to grin at her shocked face. "We don't want to attract any more attention than necessary."

He laughed as she cursed and flounced back into the house.

She made it into Franschhoek with a lot of grinding of gears and Muzi's muttering about his poor gearbox and lamenting her treatment of his SUV. Ro, trying to keep the powerful, super expensive and luxurious car on the road, ignored his running commentary and, finally, what seemed like hours later, pulled up outside a home on the leafy outskirts of the town. The house was painted a mellow cream and was set in a lush, extensive garden with what seemed to be acres planted with roses.

Ro, in shorts and a white, flowing top, cut the engine to the car and darted a look at Muzi's gray face. The man was in a lot more discomfort than she'd realized, and her heart pounded in her chest. She didn't like seeing anyone in pain, but seeing this powerful, warrior-like man gripping the seat and biting his lip made her eyes sting. She needed to get him help. And fast.

But she had no idea why they were at a private

house and not at a doctor's surgery or a hospital.
"Why are we here?" Ro asked as a pack of hounds,
of every color and breed, galloped toward the car,
barking madly.

"Don't worry about the dogs, they're harmless,"
Muzi said, his voice thready. "Hit the hooter, Ro."

The hooter? What? "Huh?" Ro asked him, not
understanding his request.

Muzi shook his head, turned his torso, and used
his left hand to hit the horn of the car. Right, in South
Africa, a horn was a hooter, a napkin was a serviette and, strangest of all, a traffic light was called a
robot. Weird.

The dogs barked again, danced around the car
and within a few minutes, a well-dressed couple appeared around the corner of the house, arm in arm.
They waved when they saw Muzi's car and the older
man released a sharp whistle that quieted the dogs
and made them sit.

Damn, she wished she could do that with her kindergarten kids.

Thinking that she was safe from the dogs, Ro exited the car and, giving the hounds a wide berth, approached the couple. "Hi. Muzi insisted I bring him
here. He's hurt."

The woman's expression immediately sharpened,
and she pulled her hand out of her husband's, her
casual stroll increasing to a fast walk. "What happened?"

"He took a fall running," Ro told her. "He's got

a bad cut on his shin, a cut on his head, I think he may be concussed. And he's dislocated his shoulder."

"Right." The woman yanked open the passenger door and glared up at Muzi. "*Really*, Triple M? This is not the way I wanted to spend my Sunday!"

Over her shoulder, Ro saw his tight smile and the fondness in his eyes for this petite but forthright woman. "Sorry, Doc."

Ro released a long, relieved sigh. Thank God, she was a doctor and Muzi would finally get some help. Ro leaned her shoulder against the back passenger door and stared down at the bright emerald grass beneath her feet. She felt like she could, finally, pull some air into her lungs.

Ro held her hand out and saw that her fingers were trembling. She'd pushed back her fear but now that there were others to help him, she felt a little dizzy. His injury could've been a lot worse. He could still be lying on that mountain, his neck broken, his head bleeding.

God...

She couldn't bear the thought. Ro wrapped her arms around her middle, forced to admit that she'd be gutted if something happened to Muzi, that he'd come to mean a lot to her in too short a time.

She'd known him for less than three weeks. How could she be feeling such a connection after so little time? It wasn't normal, not for her, anyway. She took her time with people, sussed them out and looked before she leaped.

With Muzi, she'd just dived on in...

"Cut on head and leg, a dislocated shoulder? Anything else I should know about?" the doctor briskly asked him, her sharp eyes bouncing between Ro and Muzi's injuries.

"I think that's it," Ro replied when Muzi didn't. "I think I mentioned a concussion?"

"Not concussed," Muzi stated, lifting his good hand. "Sam and John, meet Roisin O'Keefe, also known as Ro. Ro, these good people are your favorite chef's parents, John and Dr. Sam Kildare."

John Kildare, Pasco's dad, sent her a warm smile. His wife's smile was there, but cooler. "You had dinner with Muzi at Pasco's recently."

Wow, news seemed to travel at light speed in Franschhoek.

"Pasco told us, and said that he enjoyed meeting you," John explained. He placed a hand on his wife's shoulder and peered over her head to look at Muzi. "How are you doing, Triple M?"

"Hurting like a mother," Muzi admitted. "Is Pas around? I could do with his help getting out of this car."

John jerked his head and Ro turned to see Pasco, wearing a battered pair of shorts, an old T-shirt and rain boots, walking toward them, casually eating a piece of toast.

"What's the idiot done now?" he asked, not sounding remotely concerned.

Ro bristled at his casual tone. The least the man could do was show a little concern or sympathy. She moved so that she could put her hand on Muzi's thigh, giving it a sympathetic pat. He sent her a weary grin. "Much as I like your hand on my thigh, Ro, you need to get out of the way so that the moron can help me down and into the house."

Moron, idiot…okay, so this was how the old friends talked to each other. Noted.

Pasco shoved his last piece of toast into his mouth and gently nudged his mom away from the car. "I've got this, Doc," he told her. Pasco leaned across Muzi to unclip his seat belt and whistled as he caught sight of the jagged wound on Muzi's leg. "Jesus, Triple M. What the hell did you do?"

Muzi swung his legs toward the open door, his lips thin with pain. "I was on a trail run behind the house and I got a text message." His eyes connected with Ro and she knew exactly what the text message was about and she blushed. "I was trying to wrap my head around the text as I flew down the path, but I was distracted and tripped over a root, smacked my shoulder into a rock and hit my head." He glanced down at his leg. "I have no idea how I gashed my leg open."

Pasco linked his arm in Muzi's and shared his strength with him as Muzi slid out of the car. He swayed but Pasco's grip on him kept him upright. "I'll help you inside and then the doc can work her magic on you."

"And not for the first time," Sam muttered as they slowly walked to the house. "Since you are now adults, I thought I was over patching you boys up. Just goes to show that I can be, occasionally, wrong."

"Can I have that in writing?" John quipped.

"Do you want to sleep with the dogs tonight?" Doc Kildare asked her husband, the twinkle in her eye taking the sting out of her words.

Ro caught John's eye, saw his exaggerated grimace, and, caught between the urge to laugh and cry, started to giggle.

Seeing the light under Muzi's half-open bedroom door, Ro gently knocked. When she heard Muzi's command to enter, she pushed open the door.

"Hey," he said, his deep voice washing over her. He ran his hand over his jaw and glanced at the dark night beyond his floor-to-ceiling windows. "I can't believe I slept for so long. What the hell did Sam give me?"

Ro stepped into the room and rested her hand on the back of a black-and-white wingback chair. His bedroom was a study in black and white: the wall behind his head was painted charcoal, his headboard was black and snow-white linen covered his bed. Huge black-and-white photographs depicting wild, desolate beaches decorated the white wall that separated the bedroom from his dressing room, which she presumed led to an en suite bathroom. Opposite him was a huge flat-screen TV attached to the wall. He muted the sound and tossed the remote onto the bed beside him.

"How are you feeling?" Ro asked, noticing that he'd dispensed of the sling Dr. Sam insisted he wear when he left her house.

"Not too bad," he replied, crossing his long legs at the ankle. On returning home, he'd refused her help. He'd managed a shower and to pull on a pair of running shorts, but his chest was still bare. That was okay, she had no problem looking at his big body, muscles on muscles.

"Since it's Sunday, and Greta took the rest of the day off, I made a chicken salad for supper," she told him, rocking from foot to foot and trying to pull her mind off his fantastic body.

"Sounds good, but I'm not hungry," Muzi said. He patted the bed beside him. "Come here."

Ro moved to the bed and sat down on the edge, sending him a concerned look. A bandage covered the stitches in his leg and a butterfly clip held the cut on his forehead together. He had a scrape on his chin and his shoulder but, despite the hint of pain in his eyes, he looked a million times better than he did before.

"You scared me," Ro said, internally wincing at the fear in her voice.

"I'm tough. My body has taken a lot worse," he reassured, placing his hand on her bare knee. It felt good there, like it belonged. Damn, she could not be developing strong feelings for this reserved man.

She would not let herself fall for another person who would, eventually, end up hurting her. Love was a fallacy, and commitment was a concept that was, as she knew, flawed.

Muzi squeezed her knee and she lifted her head

to look into his soulful black eyes. "Thanks for your help today."

Ro nodded and half turned, putting her knee and thigh on the bed to face him. "I'm sorry I abused your fancy car."

"It'll be fine," Muzi assured her, drawing circles on the bare skin beneath the hem of her shorts.

"Do you need me to call anyone, to tell them about your accident?" she asked, trying to ignore his sparking-a-fire touch.

"No, there's no need to get Mimi upset. Or even involved." Muzi frowned. "I hope Sam didn't call her."

"Do they know each other?"

"Oh, yeah. Digby and I spent a lot of time with Pasco growing up. His folks were still living on the vineyard they own—Pasco's brother is the resident vintner now—and we were always hurting ourselves or hurting each other. Sam had to call Mimi quite a few times to inform her about my latest injury."

"And how did Mimi take those calls?"

Muzi smiled. "With equanimity. She believes that God protects the stupid. To be fair, He did that a lot because we got up to some dumb stuff."

"It was weird to see one of the world's most celebrated chefs in ratty shorts and Wellington boots," Ro commented.

Ro moved to sit cross-legged on the bed, her knee resting against Muzi's uninjured leg.

"Pas is both farmer and chef, he was probably potting around in the greenhouse. It's his way to relax."

"How do you relax?" Ro asked him.

"Working out, reading…" Heat flashed in his eyes. "Sex."

She saw the question in his eyes, knew that if she made the slightest move, she'd be naked in ten seconds and he'd be rocketing her toward an intense orgasm. But she wasn't ready, not just yet. She didn't want to sleep with him until she was very sure that she could treat him as a friend with benefits, a lovely interlude. Before she slept with him, she needed to get rid of these mushy feelings, the thoughts that something could develop between them.

Nothing could. Or would.

She knew that intellectually, but she needed to believe it, heart, body and soul. She just needed a little more time to pull herself together. She dragged her eyes off his handsome face and played with the frayed edges of her denim shorts. "I'm sorry I told Susan that we were having an affair, but I didn't know what else to tell her. She's pretty persistent."

Irritation flashed across his face. "*Persistent* is a nice word for her," he muttered, his tone bitter.

Wow, there most definitely was no love lost between them. Ro placed her elbows on the inside of her knees and rested her chin against her linked hands, ready to listen. "As you know, she's Mimi's daughter and she's on the board of Clos du Cadieux," he began.

"Mmm…"

Ro cocked her head to the side, lifting her eyebrows to get him to explain. Muzi's eyes connected with hers and slid away. His eyebrows pulled together in a deep frown and he looked away from her to the TV, and did she imagine him moving his leg so that it no longer touched hers? Oh, she didn't need to be a psychologist to tell that Susan was not someone he wanted to discuss.

A long silence stretched between them, a little uncomfortable, a lot awkward. Ro sighed, wishing he found it as easy to talk to her as she did him. With her, he just needed to look at her with those deep, intense eyes and she started to gush.

It was obvious she did not have the same effect on him.

Ro started to stand up but he gripped her knee as if he were trying to keep her in place. "It's complicated," he said, his normally smooth voice rough with emotion.

"It always is," Ro softly murmured.

"Susan doesn't like me," he stated. Ro covered his hand with hers, linking their fingers. Muzi looked down at their interwoven digits and she felt him shudder. "I should qualify that, she's never liked me. *Ever.*"

Ro frowned, trying to make sense of his statement. Looking for clarification, she tossed out another question. "You grew up with her, didn't you?"

"I told you that my grandmother worked for Mimi and I came to live with Lu when I was three. I have no memories of my life before that, few memories of my mother. I do not have the first clue who my father is," Muzi said, his voice flat and monotonous.

He sounded like he was reading from a cereal box and Ro realized that this was his way to deal with a painful subject.

If he had to explain, he'd do it but with as little fuss as possible.

"Lu was awesome and so was Mimi. Years after I came to live with Lu, Susan divorced her husband and she moved back into Mimi's mansion with her two sons. Mimi treated us all the same—I wasn't treated like her servant's son, she wouldn't countenance that. Rafe, Keane and I became like brothers."

"And Susan?" Ro asked, knowing that he'd left out a huge chunk of this story.

He stared at a point past her shoulder, and pain and anguish danced across his face and into his eyes. "She was the original Jekyll and Hyde."

"What do you mean?" Ro asked, puzzled.

His face, just for a second, revealed long-ago devastation before it settled back into his "Nothing to see here" expression. "Because of our age difference, Susan treated me like another of her sons when we had company. When we were amongst friends, or even when it was just the family, she was supersweet. But..."

She tightened the grip on his fingers, suspecting that she knew what was coming.

"But when she got me alone, she turned into a viper—a cold, angry, vicious woman."

Ah, no. Please, no.

"She told me, often, that she would do everything in her power to see that I left Mimi's house, that I was sent back to my mother's family in the Transkei, people I never met. She told me that I wasn't good enough to live at La Fontaine, which is Mimi's estate, just a few miles east of here. It's where I grew up, where Mimi still lives."

Ro felt her other hand tightening into a fist as a wave of anger bubbled up inside her. Educating kids, protecting kids was what she did, who she was, and the thought of an innocent Muzi at the mercy of a vicious adult made her want to scream.

But she knew if she reacted with anything but an empathetic expression, if she showed Muzi her anger or her sympathy, he'd take her response as pity and he'd shut down and shut her out.

"She told me that if I said anything, that if I ratted on her, they wouldn't believe me and I'd be sent away. That I would go back to poverty, that I would never be educated, that I would be alone."

Red-hot anger burned the back of her throat. Not able to say anything without revealing her anger, she gestured for Muzi to continue.

"Lu died when I was ten, Mimi adopted me and threw me an official welcome-to-the-family party. Susan hugged me, said everything she should but later on she told me, in no uncertain terms, that she would do everything in her power to ostracize me, to separate me from Mimi. Later, I realized that her intention, probably all along but definitely from the time my adoption became legal, was to separate me from Mimi's money. Mimi's enormous estate is to be split four ways, with Susan, Rafe, Keane and me as her heirs."

"And Susan doesn't like that," Ro said, proud that her voice sounded reasonably normal.

"Susan hates that. Always has, always will."

"There's more to this story, Muzi. Tell me."

He shook his head and Ro touched his masculine jaw, rubbing her fingers over his short beard. "You know my secrets, Muzi, and you can trust me with yours."

"I haven't told anybody about Susan, not even Mimi."

She could understand that. He was a proud guy. And he loved his adoptive grandmother and didn't want to cause her any pain. "Tell me everything," she insisted.

Muzi dropped his head back against the headboard and stared up at the ceiling. "The teenage years weren't so bad as I spent a lot of time at boarding school and many weekends and school holidays with friends, either at La Fontaine or at their houses. I became adept at avoiding and ignoring Susan. I went to university, and when I graduated Mimi offered me a position at Clos du Cadieux. Susan actively tried to sabotage me at work. Luckily, I learned very quickly to cover my ass and none of her machinations succeeded. Then Mimi appointed me as CEO and informed the family I would inherit her shares in Clos du Cadieux. Susan lost it."

"Publicly?"

"Hell, no. She caught me working late one night

and told me, straight-out, that there was no way she'd ever allow me to succeed at this job. And for the past few years, she's openly and actively tried to undermine and ostracize me."

Ro scratched her forehead, puzzled. "And Mimi knows this?"

"Eh…sort of. Mimi has completely retired and is no longer involved at Clos du Cadieux, She's asked me whether we've had a falling-out, but I brush it off when she brings it up."

He caught her "Why didn't you tell her?" expression and threw up his hands. "She's eighty-four years old, enjoying her retirement. What would it help to tell her that her daughter has tormented me all my life? I understand Susan, she's insecure and narcissistic and controlling but I can handle her. Rafe and I are good—he's in the States and I don't see much of him, he's doing his own thing. But losing Keane's friendship has nearly killed me. Thanks to his mother, he thinks I'm demanding and controlling and that I've been stealing from Clos du Cadieux, and Mimi, to line my own pockets."

"Why would they think that?"

"Because I have a lifestyle that exceeds the income I make from the company."

She'd been wondering about that herself. "I know I'm being nosy but how *do* you afford the very high-end art and the sculptures, the super expensive car and your fancy threads? I'm sure you earn a kick-butt salary, but you own art worth tens of millions—art that only billionaires can afford."

The corners of Muzi's mouth lifted. "I saved every penny growing up and Mimi gave me a whack of cash when I turned twenty-one. After Jack's death, your brothers vowed to have nothing more to do with their parents and, as a result, had no access to the Tempest-Vane cash.

"Radd knew this computer genius who had an idea for a new internet payment system. They used the little money they had to develop the system but soon ran out of seed money. I took my birthday money and invested in their company. When they sold, I, like them, made a fortune."

Right. Now *that* made sense.

"Mimi knows but nobody else does. I didn't think it was any of their business, specifically Susan's. But now, in Susan's and Keane's minds, the most logical explanation is that I am siphoning money from Clos du Cadieux."

Ro remembered Keane's attitude toward his mother earlier that day and shook her head. He didn't come across that way to her. Ro suspected that he was a guy caught between his loyalty to his mom and his lifelong friendship with Muzi. Oh, she wasn't going to defend him, he didn't deserve that, but she genuinely believed that things weren't as dire between them as Muzi thought.

"Why do you think Susan came here today?" Ro asked.

"I've been thinking about that," Muzi replied, looking thoughtful. "First, you've got to remember that Susan is suspicious of everything I do, all the time. She's looking for something to discredit me, a mistake I'll make to get me canned. I'm looking for a reason to get her to resign from the board. Neither of us has yet managed to dislodge the other so we're in a holding pattern. But she's looking for a gap, a way to hurt me.

"I think a couple of things, occurring at roughly the same time, caught her interest," Muzi continued. "You working at St. Urban, you living here and me leasing St. Urban land all raised her curiosity."

"But why would she come *here*?" Ro demanded.

Muzi rubbed the back of his neck. "I don't bring girlfriends home and when I go to Pasco's, I usually go with Digby or Radd, or simply on my own. Us being together was very out of the norm."

Well, well...

"Susan is clever. You're an anomaly and she'll want to find out more about you."

"She told me that I look familiar," Ro informed him. "That worries me."

"It worries me too because she knew your mom, your birth mom. In fact, they were quite good friends."

"Birds of a feather..." Ro quipped.

Muzi nodded. "If she discovers that you are Zia's biological daughter, she won't hesitate to out you. And if she finds out about a supposedly extinct cultivar on your farm, she'll find those damn vines and pull them out herself."

Awesome news. "So did I hurt or hinder our

chances of keeping all our secrets by telling her that we are having a red-hot affair?"

Muzi, for the first time that evening, smiled. "Oh, that helped. But—"

Oh, God, there was a *but*.

"But she, and everyone else—because there will be no way she'll be able to keep such juicy gossip to herself—will gossip about us and how serious we are. They'll talk engagement rings and marriage and speculate about when we plan to have children."

Ro stared at him, a little shocked and very bemused. "Just because I am, theoretically, sleeping with you? Why would they jump to such ridiculous conclusions?"

"Because I never bring women back to my hometown, and I've never, ever shared this house with a woman before. You are a very lovely exception to a long held and strictly enforced rule."

Ro didn't know what to say to that or how to react. She stared at him, conscious that her mouth was desert dry, that ripples of anticipation were running over her skin. The atmosphere in the room changed from confiding to combustible and Ro knew that if she leaned forward and placed her mouth on his, clothes would start coming off.

Her body was demanding the sexual relief only he could give her, but her mind was still throwing a hissy fit, telling her that sleeping with him was dangerous.

"I want you, Ro."

It was such a simple statement, and more powerful for being so unpretentious. He was just a man declaring what he wanted, tossing it out there to see how she'd respond.

"I want you too—" Ro admitted, feeling the heat in her cheeks.

"I can hear the *but*."

When she didn't answer—Ro was having difficulty forming her words—he sighed. "But it's too soon, but you're not ready, but I'm hurt. Which one is right?"

"All three?" Ro asked, wrinkling her nose.

"Fair enough," Muzi replied. He lifted his lips into that devastating smirk. "But, for your information, I would've still managed to rock your world one-handed."

She saw that he wasn't expecting her to take his words seriously. "Is this California king big enough for you and your ego?" she asked, her tone pert.

"Just," Muzi replied with an easy smile. "Well, if you're not going to rock my world tonight, lie down next to me, and let's watch a movie."

"What about food? You're on medication and you should eat something," Ro protested.

"Maybe later," Muzi told her, tugging her toward him. She lay her head on his shoulder and felt his big hand on her hip, holding her close. "Sci-fi, action or a war drama?"

"Historical romance, a chick flick or a tearjerker?" Ro replied, smiling as she stretched out next to him.

Muzi released a snort. "Can we compromise on a comedy?"

"Deal," Ros said, resting her hand on his flat, ridged stomach. Oh, Lord, being this close to him and not allowing herself to explore his fabulous body was pure, unadulterated torture.

She just needed to say the word and she would know if he could live up to his promise of rocking her world.

But, because she was an adult and tried to listen to her head and not her juvenile libido, she lay there and tried to concentrate on the movie.

She didn't succeed.

CHAPTER SEVEN

MUZI COULDN'T RECALL the last time a woman fell asleep in his bed and then realized he couldn't remember because it had never happened. Not once. Not even when he was younger, at university, or in the years following his studies. He far preferred to share his partner's bed, that way he could control when the evening ended.

He didn't do sex-free sleepovers, neither did he indulge in confessions. Last night he did both. He had never spent so much time explaining his past. Digby knew, or suspected, parts of it but he'd never confessed the full extent of Susan's emotional abuse.

He and Ro knew each other's secrets, and it was as scary as hell.

Muzi lay on his side and watched her sleep. Something else he wasn't in the habit of doing. Being so close he could see a tiny bump on the ridge of her straight nose, how extraordinarily long her eyelashes were and that her skin was blemish-free. When he first saw her, she reminded him of Snow White, but after a few days in her company, he knew the comparison wasn't just. She was so much more than a cardboard cutout character from an old Disney movie. She was determined, sensitive, empathetic and, best of all, nonjudgmental. And, terrifyingly, he felt the urge to spill more of his secrets.

Secrets like…while he was terrified to love, neither did he want to be alone. That, despite having the power in the wine industry he commanded, he was frightened that Susan would achieve her lifetime goal and have him sidelined and made irrelevant. Nobody, not even him, knew how far she would go.

Muzi knew that Susan never expected him to fly as high and fast as he did. And when he joined Clos du Cadieux, she'd encouraged his managers to make his life hell to avoid any accusations of nepotism. She thought he would quit. He'd done just the opposite. When threatened, he buckled down and got more stubborn. He wasn't going anywhere, and he wouldn't let an insecure and vicious woman get the better of him. But he had to do it in secret; Susan's machinations would devastate Mimi and rip the Matthews family apart. He owed it to Mimi not to let that happen.

But Muzi didn't know how to end the long-running battle.

It was early Monday morning and the sun was just breaking over the mountain. This was the time he normally went for a run or hit the gym, but with his injuries—the cut on his leg was throbbing and his shoulder still felt tender—that was out of the question. His other option was to get up and dressed and head back to the city to where a pile of work lay on his messy desk. That didn't excite him either. What he most wanted to do was to lie here and look at Ro and spend the next week discovering her delightful body.

She was, mostly, ready to go there with him, he could see it in her eyes. Normally, if a woman was even a little reluctant he would back the hell away, but Ro was a magnetic force and he was irresistibly drawn to her. He wanted her as he'd never wanted anyone before. He didn't know where to put this new, insistent, demanding desire. A part of him wanted to run away, the rest of him wanted to stay right here and hope she woke with a change of heart.

He recognized that a relationship between them was futile, that whatever was bubbling between them could not be sustained. She wasn't going to stay in South Africa, and he had no intention of living anywhere else. But more than geography separated them—he couldn't see himself handing his heart over to her, or any other woman. His birth mom had taken a piece of it when she decided that he wasn't worth keeping around, another part of his heart died with Lu. When Mimi died… No, he couldn't go there.

Love meant risk and love equaled hurt.

He'd managed to make it into his midthirties without love, or a steady relationship, someone to come home to. He was used to being alone, happy on his island. He had friends, finding a temporary lover was never a problem and being alone was safer.

Then why did being with Ro feel so damn right? It was a question he suspected would never be answered.

Muzi was about to leave the bed—they had both fallen asleep in their clothes—when Ro's hand landed on his stomach. He sucked in a surprised breath and wished, desperately wished, that her hand would move down lower. He couldn't take his eyes off her fingers, imagining them wrapped around his shaft. Just a thought caused him to turn rock-hard and it took everything he had not to release a loud groan.

He needed to leave the bed, get dressed and go back to the city.

But more than that he needed to make Ro his.

He dragged his eyes from her fingers to her wrist, up her arm, across her shoulder and onto her face. Her open, astonishing eyes were the color of old-fashioned blue ink, deep and dark and mysterious. Wide and enticing, and desperately sexy.

"Kiss me, Muzi, please."

Because he wanted to do exactly that, more than he wanted to keep breathing, he lowered his head and gently covered her mouth with his, wrapping his arm around her slim waist. He was lying on his bad shoulder and it instantly started to throb. But he didn't care how much pain this position caused his shoulder, he was kissing Ro.

And that was all that mattered.

She tasted of early morning, or honey and spice, of want and need. Cupping her face with one hand, he traced the ridge of her cheekbone as his tongue tangled with hers. He ran the back of his hand down her neck, across her shoulder, needing to feel her skin. Desire, fiery and demanding, welled up but he pushed it back.

Until she permitted him to take this further, he'd be content to feed her hot, desperate kisses and pray that gave him the green light to love her.

But even if this was all she could give him, he'd take it. Kissing Ro was better than having sex with anyone else.

Ro cupped the back of his neck and ran her hand down his bare back, over his butt. She scooted closer and pushed her breasts into his chest and he could feel her hard nipples through her bra and shirt.

Making out with her, not taking this further, was going to kill him...

Needing her entire body to be connected with his, he used his good arm to roll her onto him, her chest against his, her mound resting on his hard erection. He groaned as she ground down, her body telling him that she wanted more.

Her mouth, and brain, had yet to catch up.

Muzi ran his hand up and under her shirt, up and down her back, over her butt, sighing when the scent of her skin, citrus and flowers, flowed over him. This was the best way, bar none, to start his Monday, to start his week. Being with her was...what was the word...? Yeah. *Magic.*

He'd never used or thought of the word in the context of a woman before.

He was in more trouble than he thought.

Ro lifted her head and sent him a tremulous smile. "You okay?" he asked, seeing the sheen in her eyes.

She nodded, and he saw her swallow. Her fingers touched his short beard, wandered over his lips and traced the contours of his chin. "You are the most masculine man I've ever met. So strong, so steady."

He placed her hand over his erratic heart. "Not so steady, I feel like my heart is about to explode."

"Mine too," Ro admitted. She lifted his hand and placed it on her breast and he felt her lush roundness, the softness beneath his palm. What he couldn't feel was her heartbeat.

"Uh… Ro, your heart is on your left side," Muzi pointed out.

Ro's smile was just that side of wicked.

"I know," she whispered, placing her mouth on his. He smothered his laugh and his thumb brushed her nipple, causing her to release a little growl at the back of her throat.

He lifted her shirt, pulled down the cup of her bra and finally, finally felt her soft skin. But it wasn't nearly enough.

He wouldn't beg, it wasn't in his nature, but he found himself pulling back from her, his eyes searching hers. Hoping to see the yes he'd been longing for.

Blue met brown, desire skittered across her face, flushing her skin, and hope sparked and burst into flame. He couldn't wait a nanosecond more and released the words he'd been keeping behind his teeth. "Say, yes, Ro, *please*. Put me out of my misery."

Her creamy skin reddened in a blush, heating from the inside out and her eyes widened as she nodded. Nodding wasn't enough, he needed to hear the words. "Talk to me, Ro."

She placed her hands on his chest, ran them down his rib cage, dancing her fingers over his abs. "I want you, Muzi. I want anything and everything you can give me."

Thank God and all his archangels, angels and cherubim. Clasping her face in his hands, he pulled her down, allowing his kiss to turn ferocious. He couldn't hold back anymore, he intended to make Ro his.

Giving in to temptation was such a risk. Ro wasn't just another one-night stand, a fling. She was—could become—important. He was risking his heart again and it had taken many, many beatings in the past. He should pull back, he really should, end this now... walk away. Instead of being sensible, instead of protecting himself, Muzi rolled her over so that Ro was under him. He sat back on his haunches and pulled her upright, swiftly lifting her shirt, pulling it over her head, and throwing it to the floor. He ran his finger down her chest, circling one breast, then the other. Ro reached behind her to unclasp her bra but Muzi pushed her hands away and, with one hand, flicked open the clasp.

Ro pulled her bra down and off her arms and he looked at her, taking in her sweet breasts and rosered nipples. He touched one with the tip of his finger and watched, fascinated as it hardened under his gaze. Dipping his head, he blew on her bud and when she tensed, pulled her into his mouth. As sweet as, no, sweeter than he imagined, sheer perfection.

Muzi felt his heart bouncing off his rib cage, his lungs straining to get enough air. Sex had never affected him like this before, he'd never been compelled to immediately make her his or to slow time down to a crawl and spend eons discovering every inch of her luscious body.

He wanted to both devour and delay, ravish and ramble.

Muzi moved off her legs and slowly undid the zipper to her shorts, kissing every inch of new skin he exposed. He pushed her shorts down her legs, nipping at her hip bone and nibbling the inside of her leg before tossing them over his shoulder. She lay on his bed in a pair of pale cream panties, nearly the exact color of her skin. He allowed himself the pleasure of running his finger over her mound, between her feminine folds, and felt the dampness of her panties, reveling in the knowledge that he'd made this intriguing, lovely, complicated woman wet.

Leaving her was torture but he needed protection. Since he seldom—okay, never—brought women back here, he didn't have a stash of condoms in his bedside drawer. Remembering that he had some in his bathroom cabinet, he pulled back, smiling at her groan of disappointment.

"I need to find some condoms, baby," he told her before walking into his dressing room, and then his bathroom, glancing toward the huge corner shower, complete with two showerheads and a bench.

He could imagine sitting on that bench, Ro riding him…

But that was for later. He grabbed a strip of condoms and hurried back to her, momentarily stopping in the doorway to take her in. She looked both wanton and wonderful, turned on and temptation personified.

She was going to be his…

And he couldn't wait.

Muzi tossed the condoms near her and sent her a reassuring smile as he lowered himself back onto the bed. "Does that yes still hold, gorgeous?"

"More than ever," Ro murmured, lifting her hips in a subconscious move. "But I do wish you'd hurry up."

"Patience, sweetheart." Not that he had much himself, he was burning up with need. He knew that he could enter her, slide on home, but he wanted this first time to be something she'd remember for the rest of her life. And that meant doing something he'd been fantasizing about.

After dropping a hard, brief, openmouthed kiss on her lips, his mouth traveled down her body, over her abdomen and the fabric of her panties. She gasped and tensed. He pulled aside the fabric and circled her nub with his tongue, causing her to release a harsh scream.

Yeah, she liked that.

Impatient with the barriers, Muzi pushed her panties down her legs and placed his mouth on her core, pinning her to the bed with his hand on her stomach. Needing to give her more, he slid a finger inside her, then another, lifting his eyes to see her head thrashing against his pillow. She reached down and pushed his head closer to her and Muzi widened his fingers and sucked her harder, knowing she was close.

She turned statue still, released a long wail and he felt her gush over his fingers, buck against his mouth as she touched the sun and ignited.

He was torn between giving her more or watching her come down from her intense orgasm, and decided to combine both. Sitting up, he quickly opened a foil packet and rolled the condom down, his skin ultrasensitive.

It wouldn't take much to ignite him. Hell, Ro just needed to look at him and he'd explode.

Metaphorically. And, possibly, literally.

Lifting and widening her legs, he placed himself at her entrance and commanded Ro to open her eyes. "Is this still okay, Ro?"

She smiled at him. "What would you do if I said no...that I was done?"

He didn't return her smile. Consent was too sensitive a subject to joke about. "I'd pull back and..."

"And?" she asked, tipping her head to the side.

"Probably punch a wall," Muzi reluctantly admitted.

Ro touched his jaw with her fingertips. "I think you've been hurt enough, Triple M, so, yes, this is very okay. Or it will be when you...aargh." On hearing her yes, he'd pushed inside, and realized that she was oh so tight. For the first time in fifteen years, he wondered if he'd fit, if he'd be able to seat himself in her. He was a big guy and she was petite...

He reached down and touched her core, and pleasure flashed across her face. He felt her relax, and he sank deeper into her, groaning all the way.

Too good, there was no way he could last.

Muzi recited chemistry formulas in his head, the periodic table and the lyrics to Mi Casa's "Jika." But nothing could stop the freight train of pleasure rushing down on him.

"I can't wait...you need to come," Muzi ground out, knowing he had ten seconds, maybe less, before all hell, the good kind, broke loose.

Ro arched her back, slammed her hips up and came again, her fist to her mouth to stop the scream he knew she wanted to release.

He wanted to tell her he didn't care how loud she got, that there was no one to hear them, but that was for later, right now he was about to be smacked by pleasure and he stepped right into its path.

He'd never had it so good, was Muzi's last thought before he spiraled away.

Muzi missed work that morning. And that afternoon.

Of course, having a recently dislocated shoulder, a suspected concussion and a two-inch gash on his leg were great excuses to play hooky. Nobody needed to know—and, according to Muzi, as CEO he didn't need to explain a damn thing—that they'd spent most of the day in bed and used quite a few condoms.

Quite. A. Few.

Ro was, frankly, pretty damn exhausted.

Showered and dressed, Ro walked out of Muzi's bedroom and through his house, and after stopping in the kitchen to pick up a soda—she needed a sugar and caffeine hit—she walked onto the entertainment deck and flopped down into a chair and put her feet up on the railing.

After showering together, and indulging in some heavy petting, Muzi told her that he needed to go into his home office and check his emails and return calls, and Ro was glad for the opportunity to be alone.

She needed to think.

Best lover...check.

Best sex ever...check.

Least inhibited she'd ever been...check, check, check.

Ro sipped her drink and rested her head against the back of the comfortable chair, content to watch the sun dip behind the mountains. It was late, after six and she'd accomplished nothing today, and no, a bunch of orgasms didn't count.

Or did they?

Pulling her thoughts off Muzi and the fun they'd had—and it had been fun—she remembered that there was still so much work to do at St. Urban. The thatch needed to be replaced, she needed to get an antique expert in to value the furniture, and she suspected the place needed to be rewired.

She had weeks, months, of work ahead of her and she was glad to have an excuse to hang around Franschhoek, to be where Muzi, sometimes, was. She wanted to stay in this house, in his bed, in his arms for...hell, the longest time, probably forever.

Ro blew a curl out of her eyes, irritated with herself.

Stop fantasizing and embrace a little bit of reality, Roisin.

She had plans to make, lawyers to meet, things to do but her thoughts kept coming back to the intriguing man a couple of doors away.

Being with him had been earth-shattering, she'd adored being loved by him, she'd so enjoyed giving him pleasure...

Be sensible, Roisin. You're a reasonably intelligent woman, think this through.

She was feeling mushy, attached and emotional.

She knew that great sex produced oxytocin and that the hormone was associated with bonding, trust and loyalty. She was just experiencing a chemical storm, it didn't mean anything.

Unless it meant something...

Argh!

No, that wasn't possible. She'd known Muzi for less than three weeks, she couldn't possibly be feeling more for him than attraction. This was nothing more than rebound sex...

She wasn't the type to fall into bed, or into a relationship, quickly. When it came to her heart and emotions, she wasn't an impulsive person. It took her three months to agree to date Kelvin, another two before she slept with him. She didn't treat love rashly and didn't jump into situations that could cause heartbreak.

No, she wasn't falling in love. She was in lust... that was totally, utterly different. But if she was...

Hypothetically, she was sort of...kind of...okay with the concept and she wasn't completely freaked out. Ro tipped her head back and released a long breath. She reminded herself that she no longer knew what love meant, she'd been disappointed by Kelvin, her parents were divorcing, and Gil and Zia were the most screwed-up couple *ever*. One night with Muzi and she was prepared to ignore all rational evidence that love was a farce and dive on in?

Anyone would think that she'd banged her head, not Muzi.

Ro heard his footsteps behind her and smiled when he dropped a kiss on top of her head. He came into her direct view and Ro noticed that he was holding two wineglasses and a bottle of red.

"It's a fifteen-year-old bottle of Shiraz, from a vineyard we own," Muzi told her. "Can I interest you in a glass?"

Ro nodded, taking in his fresh pair of navy blue chino shorts, his white linen shirt and expensive flip-flops. He opened the bottle, poured an inch into each glass and handed one to her. She didn't bother to smell or swirl, causing Muzi to roll his eyes good-naturedly, and took a hefty swallow. "It's good," she told him.

"It's bloody fantastic," Muzi corrected her, sitting down in the chair next to her. Muzi dropped his head back to stare at the sunset. He sighed and when Ro looked at him, she caught his smile. "Today was a damn fun day."

"It was," Ro agreed.

"So why, then, were you looking a little lost when I came out here?" Muzi asked. His next question was typical Muzi, direct and honest. "Do you regret us sleeping together?"

Ro lifted her eyebrows. "What? *No!*"

Muzi sipped his wine and returned his gaze to the mountain and the setting sun, skepticism on his face.

She could explain, Ro thought. He'd understand. "I was just wrapping my head around the fact that I'd never had such good sex in my life, not even with my fiancé."

He shot up so fast that her head spun. "What the hell? You have a *fiancé*?"

Ro lifted her hand and shook her head. "Calm down, Triple M. It's been over for a few months."

Muzi scowled at her, his lips pulled into a thin line. "For future reference, feel free to use the prefix 'ex' whenever you mention the word *fiancé*," he muttered before sitting down again.

He sounded properly upset. "I'm sorry." She eyed him over her glass. "So, judging by your hot response, I take it that you don't sleep with women who are in committed relationships?"

He didn't need to answer, she saw his reply in his narrowed eyes and tight expression. Right, Muzi didn't poach on other men's territory. That was honorable, respectful and his response was another tick in her He'd Make a Fantastic Boyfriend column.

For someone else, obviously, but not for her. There were too many ticks in her Why This Would Never Work column to consider him as anything other than a lovely, exciting diversion.

Muzi placed his feet on the railing in front of them and watched the light changing over his lands, his tension sliding away. "What happened? Why did you guys break up?"

"He sent me a text message meant for her, saying how much he enjoyed the night they spent together. And that he liked her pink panties." Ro wrinkled her nose. "I don't own pink panties. And, big clue, I was already in Cape Town when I got the text."

Muzi muttered something underneath his breath but although she couldn't hear him distinctly, she knew it wasn't a compliment. His immediate instinct to defend her made her feel warm and squishy. She was being ridiculous.

"I presume you were devastated when he cheated on you?"

Ro nodded, then scrunched up her face, questioning her response. Had she been? She mourned the death of her dreams, the future she'd created with him, the wife she intended to be, the kids they'd have. Did she mourn him? She wasn't so sure.

"He changed my thoughts about love and relationships," Ro explained, pulling her heels up onto the edge of her chair and wrapping her arms around her bent knees. She rested her cheek on her knee as she looked at him. "Actually, everything that has happened over the past few months has changed what I thought I knew about love and commitment."

Muzi reached out, ran his hand down her arm before pulling back. "Tell me more."

"I had my life planned, we were going to get married at some point and, in time, we'd have kids. Our lives were jogging along, same old route, same old path." The wind picked up and blew a strand of hair across Ro's eyes and she irritably pushed it away.

"As it does," Muzi murmured.

"Until a hurricane whips you off said path and into a whirlwind."

"The whirlwind being your inheritance?" Muzi asked. "Bet your ex is pissed that he's not part of that action now."

"I never told him and no, my inheritance wasn't the hurricane."

"What? You didn't tell him?"

Ro shook her head.

He whistled, his astonishment obvious. "I'm sure a psychologist would have a lot to say about why you didn't trust him enough to tell him, but I digress… What was the emotional hurricane?"

Ro's chest lifted and fell. "My parents wanting a divorce. I genuinely believed they had a rock-solid marriage. I'm still in shock."

Muzi tipped his head to the side. "These things

rarely come from out of the blue, sweetheart. Are you sure that you didn't miss the signs?"

She'd thought about this, often. And hard. "Nope, I don't think I did. Every time I've seen them, they've acted like they always have, super affectionate, super touchy. I never suspected anything. Then the lawyers contacted me and told me about Gil and Zia and I went online and read all about them—"

Muzi mimicked putting a gun to his head and pulling the trigger. She managed a small smile. "Obviously, my parents' situation was still on my mind and I couldn't work out how two serial cheaters managed to stay married for so long when my seemingly hopelessly in love parents were calling it quits."

"And then you discovered that your ex cheated on you. Slap number three."

"And that's without going into the whole I-don't-know-why-my-parents-didn't-keep-me suck-fest. I no longer know what love means, what commitment is and, given that both sets of parents are incapable of both, whether I will be able to commit to anyone ever again."

Muzi's hand skimmed over her hair. "Ah, Ro."

"No words of wisdom?" Ro asked him, needing something, anything, to hold on to, to make her believe again. She wanted to, she realized. She wanted to be the woman she'd been, the one who was happy and hopeful, who was excited to be a wife and a mother. To grow old with someone.

Muzi grimaced. "Not having had a long-term relationship in my life, I don't hand out advice on love."

He looked away, obviously deep in thought. "My only contribution to this conversation is that I think you should discard anything your birth parents did or said. They were outliers, two exceptionally flawed people who found each other and who encouraged the other to be the worst version of themselves. If you discard them, who they were and what they did, you can, maybe, see your parents' marriage in a better light."

Ro kept her eyes on him, fascinated by his every word. He was thoughtful and compelling and, so far, his words were full of wisdom.

"Your parents probably agreed not to let you suspect anything about their problems, to protect you. But marriages do fail, people do grow apart, few people manage to stay married forever. People change and so does what they feel for each other."

That made sense.

"And just because they don't love each other anymore, doesn't mean that they don't love you," Muzi told her, with compassion in his eyes.

She wrinkled her nose. "I've said that to quite a few of my kids when I heard that their parents are divorcing."

"Whether you are three or thirty, it doesn't make it any less true," Muzi assured her. "As for your ex, he's an idiot who never deserved you," he added, scowling. "Did he tell you that it was an accident, that he never meant it to happen?"

"Yep."

"Then he's a double idiot. It's never an accident.

He *chose* to let it happen—he could've stopped at the first inappropriate conversation, the first time they flirted, when they first kissed—and a consequence of his choice was losing you. He bought the ticket—he gets to take the ride."

Ro sat up, dropped her legs and held out her hand for him to take, sighing when her hand disappeared in his. "Thank you. You've given me a lot to think about."

Muzi squeezed her fingers and lifted her knuckles to his mouth. "I have something else for you to think about…"

Desire, sharp and delectably fizzy, skittered through her. They hadn't been naked for more than an hour and it was far too long. "Mmm…yes, please."

His laugh was rich and deep. "I like the way you think but, sorry, I'm not offering to take you back to bed. Mimi called and she wants to see me, to see if I'm okay."

"You're very okay, I can attest to that."

He grinned. "Thank you, but Sam, the big mouth, called her and told her that she had to patch me up again. Mimi has summoned me to La Fontaine and she's ordered me to bring you. And to stay for dinner."

Ro pulled a face, not sure if she was ready to meet Muzi's grandmother. Meeting the family made her think that this…*thing*…between them was moving too fast.

"I don't know, Muzi."

Disappointment jumped into his eyes. "Her chef

cooks like a dream and she's a character but if you're not keen, I'll just head over there and have a quick drink with her." He drained his glass of wine and put it on the coffee table to his right. He glanced at his watch. "If I leave within the next ten minutes, I could be back by eight."

"And you are going back to the city in the morning?"

"Yes, I'm so behind and I have a series of meetings I have to take."

"And do you have any idea when you will be back?" she asked, trying to sound nonchalant but knowing that she missed it by a country mile.

Muzi's look was rock steady. "Is that your way of asking whether I want to see you again, to sleep with you again?"

He was so straightforward. And, after Kelvin's dishonesty and the confusion around her adoptive parents' marriage, it was a nice change. "I guess I am."

He stood up and gripped the arms of her chair, caging her in. "No promises, no expectations, but yes, I'd like to see you again. When that changes, you'll be the first to know. And, unless something major happens at work, I'll be back here Friday night."

Ro nodded, relieved. She stroked her thumb across his bottom lip and sighed when his mouth covered hers in a brief, hard kiss. Ro pouted, disappointed when he stood up and moved away to stand by the railing.

"Talking about work, your lawyers should have the lease agreement by now, can you sign it sometime soon so that my farm manager can put a cleanup crew in the lands?"

"Let him do it, I'm not going to change my mind," Ro told him, not liking the change of subject. When Muzi talked business, his expression turned implacable and a curtain fell in his eyes. He wasn't robotic but he was unreachable. And if she only had a few hours until he left her here in Franschhoek for five days she didn't want to waste a minute of that time.

She wanted to be with him. "I'll come to La Fontaine with you." She gestured to her casual shirt and shorts. "Should I change?"

He nodded. "Mimi is old-school and expects us to dress for dinner. Nothing fancy but shorts and flip-flops are not acceptable."

"Got it," Ro said, climbing to her feet. Then a thought occurred, and she hesitated. "If I go with you, your grandmother is going to believe the rumors are true."

"What rumors?"

"That we are having a red-hot affair!" Ro retorted.

Muzi smiled. "Sweetheart, we *are* having a red-hot affair. If it got any hotter, we'd both be dead, burned to a crisp."

She swatted his arm and he laughed. "You know what I mean! She'll think that there's something between us!"

Muzi placed his hand on her lower back and pushed her in the direction of the lounge. "There is something between us…" He hesitated, and Ro's heart rate sped up and her brain froze. What was he about to say? And was she ready to hear it?

"Let's take it slow, see where it goes. Right now, we are friends. Enjoying some earthshaking benefits."

Stupid girl for even entertaining the thought of more. She wasn't ready for more, and he didn't want it.

Right. They were both on the same page. That was good…

Wasn't it?

CHAPTER EIGHT

THREE DAYS LATER, Ro sat in the library at St. Urban, morosely contemplating the floor-to-ceiling shelves of books, wondering who would take a roomful of old and dusty books. And, because the Du Toit family had been überwealthy, she suspected that there were a couple of first editions on those shelves.

She needed to find someone who specialized in old books. Ro sighed and picked up her phone to add the item to her long to-do list.

Ro tucked the phone into the back pocket of her jeans and contemplated the rolltop desk standing between two long narrow windows. If the other two desks in this room were anything to go by, it would be stuffed full of old papers, crumbling bits of newspaper and ancient pens and keys.

She slapped her dusty hands together and sat down on the ancient leather chair in front of the desk. Somebody had to do it and she was here and might as well make herself useful.

And keeping busy helped the hours go faster...

The truth was, she couldn't wait for Muzi to come

home. *Home*. Ro turned the word over in her head and realized that his house did feel like home, in a way that Digby's barn conversion or even her apartment back home didn't. It shouldn't as it was filled with Muzi's possessions and she didn't have anything of her own to make it feel familiar but…

It was his favorite place and she wanted to be anywhere he was. God, she missed him. Missed seeing that half smile, hearing his deep voice, feeling safe when she fell asleep on his broad shoulder.

Wherever he was, was where she wanted to be.

She had a life back home and, if she wasn't mistaken, her lease was up for renewal. Christmas was a few weeks away and she needed to make plans to go back to LA, to be with her parents. The auction for her parents' art and collectibles would be held in the first week of January and Carrick Murphy wanted her to do a visual inspection of what she was selling, to make sure she would have no regrets later. Her teacher colleagues and college friends were demanding to know when she'd be back home… Ro cursed under her breath, feeling like the real world was intruding and that her time in this magical valley was running out. But she had so much unfinished business here.

But, really, was that true? She could hire people to sort out this house, she could talk to her lawyers about the estate via emails and phone calls, she could do electronic signatures from anywhere in the world.

No, the reason she was hanging around in Franschhoek was because Muzi was here—well, here on weekends. And she was using clearing out St. Urban as an excuse to hang around, to be with him.

Pathetic? Maybe.

Ro heard footsteps on the wooden floor outside the study and then heard an imperious voice calling her name.

Ro instantly recognized Mimi's voice and looked down at her dirt-streaked pale yellow shirt and grubby jeans. She looked, as she did most days, like she'd been rolling around in the dust.

Ro pushed back her chair and saw Mimi standing in the doorway to the library. She wore a tangerine-colored suit over a white T-shirt and funky, fashionable trainers on her feet. Designer glasses covered her eyes and she wore a gold necklace as thick as Ro's thumb.

"Dear God, child, what do you look like?" Mimi demanded, stepping into the room.

Ro greeted her before telling her that she dressed like this most days. "Not that I'm not happy to see you but why are you here?"

Mimi folded her arms across her chest. "I came to invite you to join me and a couple of friends for lunch."

Ro looked down at her dirty clothes and grimaced. "Sorry, I'm going to have to pass. Not only am I dirty, but I'm expecting the antique furniture expert to drop by soon."

"Pity," Mimi replied, walking into the room and heading for one of the long windows. The view outside was amazing, with rows of vines and the mountain looming over the farm.

"What is going to happen to St. Urban? Do you know?" Mimi demanded, turning back to face her. "I heard that Muzi signed an agreement to lease the land, and the vines, but what do you think the owner is going to do with the property?"

Was Mimi putting an emphasis on the word "owner" or was that just her imagination? Was she questioning whether she was who she said she was, an employee of the trust? Or was Ro's paranoia running away with her?

Ro wiped her dusty hand on the seat of her pants. "Muzi has expressed interest in buying the land so the owner is thinking of subdividing the property and selling the house. It's what he's done with all the other properties." Had she said too much? Was she supposed to know that much?

"He?" Mimi raised an eyebrow.

Oh, yeah, she definitely suspected something.

Mimi sent her a penetrating look. "What do you think the owner should do with this property?"

Ro joined her at the window. She shouldn't answer but she would. After all, she'd given this topic a lot of thought. "I would tell him to turn this house into an exclusive, very upmarket boutique hotel. It has over ten bedrooms, more if you converted some of the outbuildings. The place is furnished with exquisite antiques, amazing art and it's a throwback to the early 1920s."

"Carry on," Mimi instructed her.

"I'd... I'd suggest to him that he renovate the cellars and set up a tasting room and, if he was feeling brave, establish a restaurant on the property. Something ridiculously upmarket and expensive."

In her mind's eye, Ro could see the house restored, its windows gleaming, its furniture polished and the art displayed proudly. She could see guests reading in this library, sitting under the wonderfully old oak trees, sleeping in enormous beds covered with white linen, eating in a fabulous new restaurant.

It was so real she could smell the newly cut grass, the blooming roses, beeswax polish intermingled with the expensive perfume of the female guests.

Mimi took her time answering. "It's not a bad idea," Mimi eventually answered.

But was it a good one? Ro wanted to ask her—she had been, after all, a powerhouse businesswoman— but Mimi asked her another question before she could. "What's my grandson up to today?"

Uh...

Ro took a moment to switch gears. She and Muzi had spoken this morning, as they did most days. He was better than an intravenous dose of caffeine for getting her blood moving and her heart rate spiking.

"He's in meetings, I think. And he's going to have dinner with Digby and Bay tonight."

"It's been far too long since I saw Digby," Mimi complained. "He used to practically live at La Fontaine and now I have to beg him to come and see me."

Ro knew that wasn't true. Digby and Bay made a

point of visiting Mimi and called her often. "What do you mean Digby spent a lot of time with you?"

Mimi looked around for a seat and Ro pushed the leather chair over to her. Mimi sat down, crossed her legs and pulled her bag onto her lap. "Damn, I want a cigarette."

Ro glanced at her piles of old paper, horrified. "No smoking in here!"

"I gave up years ago," Mimi grumbled.

Ro leaned her hip against the rolltop desk. "You were telling me about Digby." Then she realized that she shouldn't sound so interested in her ex-boss. Damn. But this was her *brother* Mimi was talking about, she was interested in anything anyone had to say about him.

"Instead of going home, Digby spent many school holidays at La Fontaine. Basically, that meant he, Muzi, my grandsons Keane and Rafe—and that scoundrel Pasco—would terrorize the neighborhood."

Ro smiled. "I can imagine."

Mimi rested the back of her hand against her forehead, acting dramatic. "You really can't. They made me old before my time."

Mimi, as Muzi told her, spent a lot of time working so she probably didn't know half of it. "Did Digby stay with you because his parents were overseas?"

Zia and Gil had, as she read, traveled constantly.

Mimi snorted. "Partly, but mostly because they weren't interested in the boys and didn't want anything to do with them. The only reason they had children was because they were paid to do so."

What on earth was she talking about? She was about to ask when Mimi, surprisingly given her age, jumped to her feet. "I need to go. I'm going to be late."

When Mimi refused to meet her eyes, Ro knew that she was regretting her words. "Wait, hold on... explain what you meant about Digby's parents being paid to have him."

Mimi tried to wave her words away. "Nothing, I'm old and confused."

Not damn likely, Ro thought. Mimi's expression turned sly. "Why are you so interested?"

Yeah, very *not* confused.

Ro forced a smile onto her face, knowing she couldn't argue the point without raising Mimi's suspicions. "I'm just being nosy, forget about it."

Mimi nodded, sent her another piercing look before smiling. "Talking about being nosy, what exactly is happening between you and my grandson?"

Good question and one she didn't have the answer to. Friends with benefits didn't normally spend hours talking before bed and for at least a half hour in the morning before they started work. Sex buddies didn't exchange texts and voice messages or send each other silly memes and jokes.

"Is this serious or are you just knocking boots?"

How did she answer that question?

Ro could only think of one reply. "I don't feel comfortable discussing that with you."

"Pfft!" Mimi scowled and pursed her lips. Then she smiled sweetly, and Ro felt a prickle of apprehension skitter up and down her spine.

"I like you. I do."

But…? Because there was a glittery pink and purple neon *but* heading her way.

"But know this, if you break his heart, I will break you."

All righty, then.

Muzi stood in Digby's office at The Vane and scowled at his two best friends. He should be back in his office, putting out fires, but here he was, arguing with the Tempest-Vane brothers, trying to convince them to tell Ro the truth about why she was adopted.

Earlier in the day, he'd taken a break between meetings and frowned when he saw a couple of missed calls from Ro. When he picked up his voice messages, she told him that Mimi—his gossipy, garrulous grandmother—told her Gil and Zia had been compensated for having children. Was Mimi right, she'd demanded to know. She was also, she told him, going to call her brothers to get to the bottom of Mimi's bizarre claim.

"It will hurt her, Muzi," Digby said, after slamming his fist against his desk. "How do you think she's going to feel hearing that our parents gave her up for adoption because they weren't going to get paid the millions they did when they produced a boy?"

He understood their concern. But what Ro's brothers didn't realize was that she could handle it. That she was strong. Oh, it would hurt, but it wouldn't make her buckle or bend.

Ro was tougher than that. She was...

She was amazing. Strong and sexy and sensible and...*lovely*. She was everything he'd ever want in a woman. Intelligent, empathetic, hardworking and independent.

Sweet and so heart-stoppingly sexy. And stubborn...

And because she was stubborn, she would hound them, and him, until she had an answer to the question of Gil and Zia being paid to have kids.

Bloody Mimi and her big mouth.

Muzi ran his hand over his jaw, recalling the puzzled looks Mimi sent Ro when they dined with her earlier in the week. She looked at Ro as if she couldn't place her and had mentioned, on at least two occasions, that she looked familiar.

To him, she looked like a feminine version of her brothers but no one had yet, as far as he knew, commented on the similarities between Ro and the Tempest-Vane siblings. Muzi had also seen pictures of a young Zia and Ro looked like a carbon copy of her birth mother.

Mimi would eventually make the connection, would figure out that she was a Tempest-Vane but he knew that if he asked Mimi to keep her identity a secret, she would.

Mimi could be a vault when she needed to be.

But that was a problem for the future. They had to resolve the one in front of them first.

"I'm heading up there tomorrow and she is going to bug me for an explanation," Muzi said, slapping his hands against his hips and scowling. He knew that he looked big and intimidating but he didn't, sadly, scare the Tempest-Vane brothers.

"I'm not lying to her, guys," Muzi said, annoyed at the desperate tone in his voice. "Please don't ask me to do that."

Digby placed his palms flat on his desk and glared at Muzi, his expression thunderous. "What is going on between you?" he demanded.

God only knew.

They talked, a lot. They discussed movies and books and covered all the subjects couples talked about when they wanted to get to know each other. But they also ventured into deeper territory and shared their fears and childhood memories, both good and bad. He told her about how he saved every penny he was gifted or earned, how terrified he was of Susan's threat coming true, of him being alone. And poor.

She told him that she often felt on the outside of her parents' marriage, that they were so into each other and seemed to, occasionally, forget about her.

He told her about his travels, his daredevil adventures with Digby, and she told him how much she missed teaching and her students.

He couldn't define what they were, but they were more than friends. Ro had crawled under his skin, into his heart. He'd told her more than he'd told all his friends, and Mimi, combined. She knew his fears and his failures and his insecurities, the jagged pieces he never revealed to anyone. The thought, and realization, terrified him.

She was not only his lover, but she was also his best friend. Yet she was supposed to be returning to the States soon, leaving him behind.

He wanted to ask her to stay but couldn't give her a good enough reason to do that. He wouldn't, couldn't commit to her—he was not prepared to throw himself off that cliff and not have her catch him—yet it wasn't fair to ask her to stay if they were going to simply continue their sex-based friendship. She deserved more...

She deserved *everything*.

But he couldn't give her what she wanted. He wasn't brave enough to ask her to be his family, to have his kids...not without an unbreakable guarantee and, as far as he knew, relationships didn't come with warranties.

"Well?" Radd demanded, pulling Muzi back to their conversation.

He and Ro were adults, they didn't owe anyone an explanation. Not even her siblings, the men he considered to be *his* brothers too. This was, and always would be, between them.

"None of your business," Muzi ground out, heading toward the door before turning and raising his index finger to point it at Digby, then Radd. "Tell her. I'm not going to lie to her."

Muzi closed his office doors on his words, hoping that he was right to insist that her brothers tell her. And that Ro could handle more awful news.

On Friday, the day after her conversation with Mimi, Ro worked at St. Urban, trying to decide whether she should make the drive to Cape Town to confront her brothers. When she'd called them, both Radd and Digby professed innocence about Mimi's comment, with Radd stating that Mimi was old and confused. Digby told her that all sorts of wild stories and rumors circulated about their parents and, if she wanted to remain sane, it was best to ignore them.

Ro knew they were both lying.

Mimi wasn't confused and her offhand comment wasn't the result of unfounded gossip. She'd heard her brothers' swift intakes of breath when she raised the subject, heard the forced note of cheer as they tried, using a lot of fake casualness, to dismiss her question. There was something to Mimi's comment, she was sure of it. She'd tried to call Mimi, to ask her to join her for a coffee at one of the many cafés in town but, curiously, Mimi was ducking her calls.

She needed to know, Ro thought, carrying a box of papers toward the skip that stood under the old oak tree. It was an important piece of the missing puzzle, something that would greatly contribute to her understanding of her birth parents. But nobody was talking.

Even Muzi, when she'd raised the subject with him over the phone, switched subjects. The more they fudged, the more determined she was to find the truth.

And she would—*somehow.*

Ro heard a powerful engine and turned around to watch Muzi's car navigate her still bumpy driveway. She glanced at her watch, happy he was, by her count, at least five hours early.

Her heart bounced off her ribs as she dropped the box into the skip and, yanking off her work gloves, ran to meet him, thoroughly overexcited. Damn, she needed him. Preferably naked and on top of her.

Muzi, clutching a stack of papers in his hand, exited the vehicle and Ro threw herself at him. He wrapped his free arm around her and found her mouth, his tongue immediately sliding past her lips. Ro sank into him, pressing her breasts against his chest, pulling his shirt from his tailored suit pants to find his skin.

God, they'd only been apart for five days but she'd *missed* him.

Muzi spun her around and pinned her to the back passenger's side door, papers fluttering to the ground when his hands slid up her rib cage to cover her breasts. His thumbs brushed over her already hard nipples and he pushed his erection into her.

Well, it seemed like he'd missed her too.

They kissed and groped for the longest time, long drugging kisses that made her forget her name and it was Muzi who eventually pulled back to rest his forehead against hers.

"Hi," he murmured.

"Hi back," Ro lazily replied, loving the way there wasn't space enough for a paper between them. "Did you miss me?"

Muzi pushed his hips into hers and she sighed at how hard he was. "What do you think?" he murmured, dropping light kisses on her jaw.

Ro caught his chin and tried to bring his mouth back to hers but he shook his head. "Seriously, if we don't stop, I'm going to take you right here and right now."

The idea of making love outside made her shudder with pleasure. "I'm okay with that."

Muzi grinned. "I'm not because my farm manager has a crew in the fields, and they are going to be breaking for lunch soon."

Damn, Ro thought. "There are numerous bedrooms inside, most of which have beds."

Muzi grimaced. "That would be like making love in a dust storm." He kissed her nose and pulled back. "We're adults, we can wait."

"Being an adult sucks," Ro grumbled.

Muzi bent down to pick up the papers he'd dropped. He waved the papers under her nose. "Here's your copy of the signed and notarized lease between Clos du Cadieux and the trust."

Ro squinted down at the papers and nodded. More paper, she was already swimming in the stuff. "I'll get it from you later."

As Muzi opened his car door to toss the lease onto his passenger seat, Ro noticed a group of men coming up from the field. She blushed. If she and

Muzi hadn't slammed on the brakes, the poor men would've had to bleach their eyeballs.

Good call, Triple M.

"How is your day going?" Muzi asked her, loosening his silver tie—Hermès?—and rolling up the sleeves of his deep gray button-down shirt. He wore a different watch today, a vintage Rolex.

"Good," Ro answered, tucking her hands behind her, between her butt and the car, so that she didn't reach for him. "I spent some time this morning drawing up a list of steps I would have to take to turn this into a boutique hotel."

She'd told him about her plans for the house and he'd listened but not given her much encouragement one way or the other. "You haven't given me your opinion on whether you think it's a good idea or not."

Muzi wore his implacable expression, the one she was coming to hate. She couldn't read him when he pulled on his "You can't see into me" cloak.

"I don't have an opinion on the house, it's yours to do what you wish." She started to protest but he cut off her words by holding up his hand. "My biggest question is how you are going to manage the process from the States?"

What was he talking about? Of course she couldn't do this from the States. She'd have to be here, staying in Franschhoek, preferably in his house. "Obviously, if I decided to do this, I'd have to stay." Not wanting to scare him, she sought to reassure him. "For at least another six months, maybe a year."

A tiny frown appeared between his eyebrows. "But then you'd go back, right?"

What did he want her to say? That, yes, she'd go back? Or, no, she wanted to stay here forever? She didn't know so she remained silent, hoping he'd help her out by giving her a hint on what he wanted. Where he saw them going.

She hated being in limbo, not knowing which way they were heading. She coped better with people, and life, when she knew where she stood, how to get from point A to point B. She wasn't a person who could waft in the wind.

Sometime soon, she and Muzi would need to define their relationship so that she could envision the road ahead. But did she have a right to ask that of him when she didn't know what love was, what it meant or what it could be? She could love him, she admitted. Probably did already. But did that matter when she couldn't define where and how to place that love, where and how to let it grow?

Damn, she was so confused. But she was sure of two things: she and Muzi needed to talk—sometime soon—and that she only wanted to stay in South Africa if she could be with him.

Living in this country, without him, would be untenable.

Muzi watched her eyes, saw the confused thoughts jumping in and out of all that dark blue. He could, if he was stupid enough to do so, take some comfort in the fact that she seemed to be as rattled by what was happening between them as he was, but it didn't negate her words.

She might want to delay her departure, but she would, at some point, now or later, go back to LA. Her life was there.

His was not.

"I'd appreciate your input on whether it's feasible to turn this place into a guesthouse or boutique hotel, Muzi," Ro stated, her tone subdued but her voice clear.

Muzi gave himself a mental slap. He was a businessman and she, at the very least, was his friend. A friend who didn't have any business experience where he had lots.

Muzi sighed and turned to look at the house. The contractors had painted the exterior, and the windows were clean, and the house seemed happier, more cheerful. Man, he was losing it if he was giving inanimate objects human traits.

"This valley already has a lot of hotels, Ro, so it would have to be pretty special."

Ro nodded. "It needs something to set it apart from the rest, something to encourage people to stay here. So many wine estates have restaurants and coffee shops, galleries and gift shops, I don't want to imitate them."

An idea popped into Muzi's head, born out of a conversation he'd had earlier in the week with Pasco, who'd bitched to him about having to return to New York. Pas was tired of working sixteen-hour days and, having won every award he possibly could, was over the finicky, stressful world of fine dining in New York. He wanted to kick back and relax...

Would Pasco consider returning to Franschhoek and opening a smaller version of his NYC restaurant here? At St. Urban?

He could only ask. But he wouldn't mention his idea to Ro, not until he spoke to Pasco. He didn't want to get her hopes up.

"Let's sit down this weekend and draw up a business plan, crunch the numbers," Muzi suggested.

"I have no idea how to draw up a business plan," Ro reluctantly admitted.

"I do," Muzi assured her. He turned to face her and gently gripped her chin and jaw with the fingers of one hand. "But that will only be after I've had my way with you, several times."

There was no way he could concentrate on doing anything pertaining to business until he'd rid himself of the gnawing need to have her under him, over him, up against a wall.

First things had to come first.

"I can live with that," Ro said before lifting her mouth to receive his hard, brief and openmouthed kiss. Thinking that there was no time like the present, he spoke again. "Shall we get going, then?"

Ro glanced at her watch and shook her head. "I wasn't expecting you this early and the gardening crew is working a half day. They should be done in fifteen minutes or so. You go home and I'll lock up behind them and I'll join you there as soon as I can."

He shook his head. "I'll go and inspect the vines

while we're waiting," Muzi told her, happy to be in the fresh air, feeling the sun on his face.

Ro nodded. He was about to turn away when she put her hand on his arm to stop him. When he looked down into her face, he saw the determination in her eyes. "Muzi, I also need to talk to you about us, where we are going and about what Mimi said. Also, I think she suspects who I am."

Damn, he'd been hoping to dodge both those bullets. No such luck.

"Even if Mimi did suspect, she'd respect your privacy and would never tell anyone. But if you are so worried about being outed, why don't you get ahead of it and issue a press statement to tell the world who you really are?"

"And have them hound me and dig into my life? Radd and Digby accept me, that's all I ever wanted," she retorted before flinging up her hands. "Look, I'm not an idiot, I presume that someone at some point will connect the dots but I'm not releasing any information before I need to."

Fair enough.

"Now, what did Mimi mean when she said that my parents were paid to have kids?" Ro asked him, *again*. Damn, he'd hoped his question about her true identity would distract her, but it hadn't worked.

"Can you not let this go, Ro?" Muzi asked, a little desperately. This was between her and her brothers, he shouldn't even be involved in this!

Ro folded her arms across her chest, defiance in her eyes. And all over her face. "Would you?"

Of course he wouldn't. Muzi sighed. He yanked his phone out of his pocket and pulled up Digby's number. The phone rang twice before he heard his friend's cool voice. Right, Digby was still pissed. That was okay, he was pissed too. No doubt they'd get over it at some point.

Muzi locked eyes with Ro as he spoke into the phone. "She wants to know, and I told you I wouldn't lie for you."

"You can't tell her," Digby insisted.

"Then you tell her!" Muzi told him and, not waiting for an answer, passed his phone to Ro. She held it up to her ear and held out her other hand to him, needing the contact.

Muzi linked her fingers in his and watched as the color drained from her face, her eyes turning a dark and tumultuous blue. From where he stood, he could hear Digby's voice but not his words. Still, judging by Ro's reaction, he assumed Digby was telling his sister the abysmal truth.

Her birth parents only kept her brothers because they were paid a couple of million for each son they bore and—*snort!*—raised. Gil's Tempest-Vane grandfather hadn't thought girls were worth that amount of money, or any, so there was no financial reward for producing a girl.

And, to Gil and Zia, why keep her around if there wasn't anything in it for them?

When the call ended Ro dropped her hand, stared down at the screen before eventually handing him his phone. Seeing the devastation on her face, he started to pull her into him, needing to comfort and reassure her, but she stepped back abruptly, lifting her hands to ward him off.

"No, please, don't." She pushed her hair away from her face and held it back, her eyes extraordinarily dark in her ghostlike face.

Digby and Radd were right, this had been a bad idea. Ro was knocked sideways, emotionally drawn and quartered. What the hell had he been thinking?

"Tell me how I can help you, Ro," Muzi pleaded, wishing she'd let him hold her.

"I need to be alone, Muzi," Ro said, her voice hollow. "I need to digest this, wrap my head around it."

"I'll wait—"

Ro dropped her hands and violently shook her head. "No, go home. Please!"

"I don't want to leave you alone, sweetheart," Muzi told her, sounding and feeling desperate.

"But that's what I need, Muzi," Ro replied, and he heard tears in her voice. One tear hovered on the rim of her right eye, but she blinked rapidly and it went away. Muzi watched as she sucked in a deep breath and straightened her spine.

She wouldn't let him, or anyone else, see her cry.

She had her pride, as did he. And if she needed time alone, he would respect her wishes and give her what she wanted.

Later, he'd hold her. For as long—fifteen minutes or for the next year—as she needed him to.

CHAPTER NINE

Ro was still trying to make sense of the bombshell Digby dropped nearly five hours later.

Over the past couple of months, on reading or hearing something about her parents, Ro often thought that she'd heard the worst of what they were capable of. Then a new story would surface, one she hadn't heard before, and she'd be shocked to her core, thinking that *this* had to be the worst of them…

But this was, absolutely, as low as they, or anyone, could go.

She'd been tossed aside, dispersed of because she was a girl and didn't come with the right equipment. Holy, holy hell.

Now she understood why neither her brothers nor Muzi had wanted to explain Mimi's odd comment. They hadn't wanted to hurt her. But she'd pushed and pushed and here she sat, in the corner of the low stone wall, hurting.

She'd been looking for reasons to like Gil and Zia, to understand them, to find justifications for their revolting choices. But, with this soul-shredding news, she was forced to accept that Gil and Zia were twisted, probably evil, utterly narcissistic and a waste of oxygen. And she carried their genes.

Dear God, the knowledge hurt.

The fact that they thought she wasn't worth keeping hurt. And knowing that she loved Muzi and that he clearly didn't love her...

Hurt worst of all.

Ro stood up, brushed the seat of her pants and told herself to pull herself together. Muzi never promised her anything other than a fling, her birth parents did her a favor by giving her up for adoption—her parents adored her and gave her a wonderful life—and her roller-coaster life would even out, hopefully sometime soon.

Ro leaned her butt on the concrete wall and stretched out her legs. She needed to go home, have a shower, drink a glass of wine and spend time with Muzi.

She didn't know how much time she'd have with him and sitting here, moping, wasn't productive.

Or fun.

Ro heard her phone ring and pulled it from the back pocket of her shorts, wrinkling her nose when she saw it was Kelvin video calling her. She'd been ducking and diving his calls for ages, maybe she should just answer, speak to him and move on.

She swiped the screen and their eyes connected through the power of technology.

"Hi, how are you?" Look at her, being so adult.

"I'm good," Kelvin replied, a smile lifting his lips.

He had a great smile, Ro admitted, but it seldom reached his eyes. Muzi smiled less often but she always caught the laughter in his eyes, the amusement turning his brown-black eyes luminous. His smile could power the sun.

And God, those dimples.

Muzi's, not Kelvin's. Kelvin didn't have dimples.

Kelvin peered into the screen, his eyebrows pulling together. "Good grief, you are filthy, what on earth have you been doing?"

Ro turned the screen and panned her camera over the outside of her house before turning it back to face her. "I'm renovating this house."

"Why?" Kelvin asked, horrified. His distaste amused her. Kelvin did not like to get his hands dirty.

Ro jumped up backward to sit on the veranda wall, the heels of her trainers banging against the rough wall. She shrugged. "It's a job."

He nodded. "You must be running low on your savings by now. Isn't it time you came home?"

If he only knew. "I'm thinking about it," she told him. She was thinking about many things, including how to incorporate a big, bold African man into her life. And how to get him to include her in his.

"Why did you call, Kelvin?"

He rubbed his hand behind his neck, looking contrite. "I wanted to say that I'm genuinely sorry. I messed up but I want you back."

"Yeah, you did," Ro said. "And I'm sorry, but I'm not interested."

"I made a mistake, Ro. We can make this work, I know we can."

How to get through to him? Ro thought about and discarded a few options and decided to hit him with the truth. "Kelvin, I don't love you anymore. I don't know if I ever did. I don't know what love is, what it means for me, how it's supposed to be. But what I do know for sure is that you are not it, that you no longer have a piece of my heart."

Oh, God, were those tears in his eyes? "Does that mean that you've found someone who does own a piece of your heart?"

She could lie and tell him no, but she couldn't deny what she felt for Muzi anymore, the feelings bubbling and burning, rippling and roaring. Neither did she want to, because those crazy feelings were demanding to be explored, to be *acknowledged*.

"I have found someone new. I don't know if I'm in love with him but I'm pretty damn close," she admitted. "I'm feeling like I am standing on the sharp edge of a knife, that one misstep will slice me in two. He has the power to hurt me, Kel, in a way that you never did."

Ro stared at her grubby shoes, the streaks of dirt on her jeans. "You cheated on me and it pissed me off, I was so mad at you."

"You had—have—a right to be. I was an idiot," Kelvin said.

Ro smiled. "That's exactly what Muzi called you." Ro turned, propped her phone against the wall, lifted her legs and placed her chin on her knee, her eyes on the small screen. "The point is…my pride was hurt but your betrayal didn't touch my heart. I shrugged it off. I shouldn't have felt so little, been so blasé. I'm not trying to hurt you but Muzi makes me *feel*, Kel, in a way you never did. He makes my skin tingle and my heart feel like it's going to jump out of my chest. He makes me think and laugh and when I'm around him, I feel the best version of myself."

"And if he cheated on you?" Kelvin asked her, his tone subdued.

The idea was too horrible to contemplate. She bit her lip, her eyes brimming as sadness and devastation flowed over her. "He'd break my heart. He has the power to emotionally chop me up in little pieces, to rip me in two. I've never had such a strong reaction to anyone in my life and I doubt I ever will again." Ro released an unhappy, tiny laugh. "He's phenomenal."

"And you're telling me that you're *not* in love with him?" Kelvin said, sounding unconvinced.

"I'm trying not to be, I'm trying to protect myself," Ro told him, knowing it was true. "I'm trying to do anything and everything I can to stop myself from tumbling into this crazy situation I don't understand, one I can't figure out and most definitely can't control. Feeling like this is terrifying."

"I'm sorry I couldn't be that person for you, Ro."

She nodded, not knowing what else to say. Kelvin cleared his throat, sat back in his chair and touched the perfect knot in his tie. "I went to see your folks, by the way."

Ro knew him well enough to recognize that he'd closed the door on their emotional conversation. "They look pretty relaxed for a couple who are divorcing. Honestly, I really thought they'd last forever."

"You and me both," Ro told him. "Do you think there's any chance of them reconciling?"

Kelvin frowned. "Ro, they've legally filed, their documents are in the system. I've split their assets and they've put their house on the market. Their marriage is over."

So they were going ahead with their divorce. It was more than they'd told her. Then again, she couldn't complain about their lack of openness, she was keeping a couple of big and bold secrets herself.

"I'm sorry," Kelvin said, sounding sincere.

"Yeah, me too," Ro whispered.

Kelvin cleared his throat and gestured to his desk. "I need to get some work done. Thanks for taking my call." He looked down before forcing his eyes back to her face. "Again, I'm sorry. I'm sorry we didn't work out, and I'm so sorry for cheating on you. I wish you a good life, Ro."

It was over, they were fully done and from this moment on, Kelvin would be a memory. "You too, Kel."

"I hope he makes you happy, kiddo, you deserve it."

Ro's smile wobbled. "I hope so too. Be happy, Kelvin." Feeling a tear slide down her face, she jabbed her finger on the red button and Kelvin's face disappeared. And just like that, he was gone. Permanently.

Ro rested her cheek on her knees and watched as Muzi crossed the verandah to sit next to her on the wall. He'd arrived as she took the call and she'd known he was standing there, just around the corner. She always knew where he was, felt his energy, could sense his eyes on her.

And maybe that was why she'd been so open with Kelvin, said the things to him that she couldn't say to Muzi, knowing that her emotional words would force them to confront their feelings, to jolt them out of this holding pattern they were in. To move them along.

To get them from point A to point B.

Beside her, Muzi stretched out his long legs. Ro didn't prod him, knowing that he'd speak, eventually.

"You knew I was there," Muzi stated, his voice low.

"Yes. I was waiting for you, I knew you'd come back to check on me, to comfort me and to tell me that my birth parents' decisions have nothing to do with me," Ro replied.

"And you used your ex as a conduit to talk to me."

His tone was so bland that Ro couldn't decide whether he was angry or not. Ro felt his eyes on her face and lifted her head, forcing herself to meet his eyes. "I never planned it, he asked me the question and I responded with the truth."

"Next time, say what you need to say to my face, Roisin."

Ro winced. Yep, okay. Noted. She waited for him to rip into her some more, but he just rubbed the back of his neck, then the side of his jaw. He was feeling uncomfortable, Ro realized, unsure. Good, she wasn't feeling too confident herself.

"You said that I have the power to rip you apart. Is that true?" he finally spoke again, his voice as deep as the night.

Right, they were going to do this. Ro sucked in a breath and held it, suddenly wishing she could backtrack. But Muzi, she knew, didn't dodge or duck, he faced situations head-on. And she'd shoved theirs into his face.

In a few minutes she'd either be sinking or swimming, dancing or drowning.

"Yes," Ro whispered.

"You have the same power, Ro. More than anyone I've ever known."

She knew that and was humbled that she could affect this strong resilient man in such an emotional way. "So let's not hurt each other, Muzi," she softly suggested. "Let's promise each other that we won't."

She heard the clang of desperation in her voice, the way her voice rose and fell, coated with anxiety.

"I can't promise that, Roisin. You can't either."

Sadness coated his words, and Ro's heart plummeted to her feet. Her intuition told her that this wasn't going to end well.

"You are braver than I am, Ro, willing to wade into these dark waters even though you don't understand them and have no idea how to navigate them, how to protect yourself."

She held her breath, knew what was coming next.

"But I'm not that brave, not that strong. I don't trust love to stick around, I *can't* trust it. I lost my mother when I was three, my grandmother when I was a young kid. I lived under the threat of losing my family my entire life. I will, hopefully not anytime soon, lose Mimi. I survived my childhood, I didn't let Susan break me and when Mimi's time comes to move on, I'll mourn her, and I'll miss her. But I'll cope."

Ro held her breath, waiting for the hammer to fall. "But I can't survive losing you, Roisin. Like you, I am standing on that knife-edge, ready to fall. But I'm not going to do that. I *can't* and I *won't*. I'm going to be sensible and back away, while I still can."

Muzi stood up and dropped a kiss on the top of her head. "I could love you, Ro, we both know that. And yeah, I'm scared of being hurt. But more than that, I can't bear the thought of doing something to hurt you. I would rip anyone in two who caused you one tear…"

He hesitated, took a breath and forced the words out. "But the hell of it is, I know that I have the power to hurt you the most, to hurt you *again*. Nobody gets to do that, Ro, especially not me. I hope you find love, Ro. I hope you find a man who can give you everything you want, everything you need, what you deserve."

She didn't want anyone else, she wanted *him*. But

Ro was old enough, and wise enough, to know her wants and needs didn't matter. She couldn't demand him to be brave, to take a chance, to love her as she did him.

Love, not given freely and courageously, wasn't love at all. So Ro bit her lip and watched him walk away.

And slowly, so very slowly, she started to sink, knowing that she was about to, mentally and emotionally, drown in the sadness enveloping her.

CHAPTER TEN

Ro TOSSED STAINED and ratty blankets into the skip, once again dirty and dusty. The cleaning crew had been back yesterday, and they'd swept and vacuumed the inside of the property, mopped the floors and cleaned the windows but she still found ways to get filthy.

Today she was sorting through the piles of linen. The finely embroidered tablecloths, stitched by her great-grandmothers, would be hand-washed and placed into plastic containers to protect them from moths and other vermin, but sheets and duvets and stained tablecloths were all going in the skip.

She wished she could toss out her problems as easily, but life didn't work that way.

More than a week had passed since that night she couldn't stop thinking about. The night Muzi left, she'd curled up on a couch in the library and white-knuckled it, thinking that this was true heartbreak. She'd cried until a soft dawn broke over the mountain.

The next day she'd forced herself to swing by

Muzi's place to collect her stuff. He wasn't there, Greta told her, and the housekeeper had been instructed to pack up Ro's bags.

Refusing to cry—knowing that if she started again, she might not stop, *ever*—she went into Franschhoek, picked up food and fresh linens, and organized to have a bed delivered to St. Urban. She hadn't left her property since.

She wasn't eating and she wasn't sleeping, and was, she decided, a walking, talking zombie. She'd been so desperate to sleep last night that, sometime around midnight, she decided to take a long walk through the vineyards, hoping the fresh night air would help her to get some rest.

Leaning against the skip, she remembered her walk through the section of the vines that had been cleared by Muzi's farm crew, the moonlight so bright she hadn't needed a torch to navigate her way. When she came to the property boundary she'd video called her mom and was pleasantly surprised to find her dad with her.

She hadn't spent a lot of time on pleasantries, she'd simply jumped right in and asked them what was happening with their divorce.

"We're going ahead with it," her mother told her, "and we expect it to be finalized within a few months."

"We are good friends, Ro, and we intend to stay that way," her dad assured her.

"And you will always be our daughter. We've just

changed, moved on from each other," her dad added. "Love doesn't always last forever, pumpkin."

"But it should, I want it to! I need to believe that love can last forever!" she'd shouted, tears on her cheeks. "I want to love someone and to *know* that it will last forever. Look, I know that I am being overly romantic and highly unrealistic," she continued. "I know that having a relationship that lasts a lifetime is something rare and wonderful and the chances of it happening to me are extremely unlikely."

"You and Kelvin—"

"Kelvin and I are over." Ro sat down between the vines and watched the moonlight dance across the leaves. After taking a deep breath, she told her parents that she was the biological daughter of two of the most dysfunctional people the world had ever seen and that she'd inherited their fortune.

She told them she was obscenely rich, that they had to keep her identity a secret and that she'd decide, when the time was right, to reveal to the world that she was the long-lost Tempest-Vane heir. Or she might not. She'd see what worked best for her sometime in the future.

Oh, and that she'd fallen for another man. Her explanations took time, and it was over twenty minutes before she could return to her point about relationships.

"If my decent, lovely parents can't make their relationship work, what chance do I have? My parents, my real parents, the two people who made me believe that happily ever after in love is possible, are splitting up. My birth parents routinely cheated on each other but stayed married. My fiancé cheated on me two weeks after I left home, and I've fallen in love with a man who's everything I want but he's commitment-phobic and has abandonment issues."

She could see the long look her parents exchanged—saw the love in their eyes—and a few of the many knots in her stomach eased.

"We loved each other wildly, intensely, wonderfully," her dad said, emotion coating every word. "Do I regret that? Not for a second. Your mom has given me so much pleasure and I've loved every moment with her. And you were a gift from heaven above."

"We loved each other, Roisin, and we still do. It's just…changed," her mom said, resting her temple on her dad's shoulder. "Will that happen to you? With this man or someone else? I don't know, life and love don't come with any guarantees. But do we think you should walk away from love, now or in the future, because we're getting divorced and your birth parents were lunatics? No, that's…*nuts*."

"You decide your future, who you love and how you love that person," her dad told her, sounding a little cross. "You don't get to walk away from love because of something that might or might not happen in the future."

Shocked by her normally easygoing father's harsh words, she'd nodded. Growing up, her mom was the whip-cracker but when her dad waded in, she never argued. "That's all very well, Dad, but he won't let himself love me."

And that's what it came down to: she might be prepared to take the risk of loving him, to see where this went but a relationship needed two people to be courageous, to take a chance, to make it work.

Muzi wasn't prepared to put any skin in the game and she couldn't force him to. Love wasn't love when it was demanded or coerced.

Muzi wouldn't allow himself to love her and she needed to accept that. But, God, it *hurt*.

When they disconnected, Ro remained seated on the damp grass, thinking of her dream to be the center of a man's world, the glue that held a family together. But the only man she could see herself being with was Muzi. And he didn't want her...

Feeling the burn of tears—she'd never cried so much in her life—Ro climbed to her feet, her attention caught by the sheen of moonlight on the leaves of the vines. She touched a leaf on her left, smiled, and looked right...

The moonlight looked different on those leaves. Ro frowned, thinking that she was going mad. Rubbing her eyes, she inspected the vines again and stepped away to look at them from another angle. The vines on her right definitely didn't reflect the moonlight in the same way the vines on the left did.

And were the vines on the right a little bigger, with bigger veins running through them? In the moonlight, they looked dissimilar.

Ro decided that they were...

Could these subtle differences mean that she'd found Muzi's precious cultivar? She didn't want to get his, or her, hopes up but...

Maybe. Just maybe.

If she couldn't give him her love, at least she'd be able to give him the gift of securing his position in Clos du Cadieux. It was something, she supposed.

Nine long-ass days after last seeing Ro, Muzi strolled into Pasco's at lunchtime and found an empty seat at the bar, wondering if noon was too early to get slammed.

He lifted his hand to his head and remembered that he'd just managed to get rid of remnants of last night's hangover and he didn't know if his poor head could take another beating. Tomorrow was Monday, and he had a board meeting, where he expected to take flak for leasing land comprised of Merlot vines.

He planned to tell the board that, according to his research, he was convinced a good portion of those vines weren't Merlot, and in a few years, Clos du Cadieux would launch an exceptionally rare, award-winning wine on the market.

They'd be excited to hear that, and pretty damn pleased with him. And as soon as their excitement bubbled down, he'd make another announcement...

They needed to choose between him or Susan. If they wanted him to run Clos du Cadieux and to bring a new wine to the market—an expensive, rare, hugely profitable wine and one only he could produce—Susan needed to step down.

Or else he would resign. And, as per the contract he'd signed with Ro, the St. Urban vines went with him. Thank God that she'd insisted on including that clause in the agreement—she'd only wanted to deal with him and nobody else—it gave him a safety net. If they did choose Susan over him, he'd still have the vines and could still bring a wine made from the C'Artegan cultivar to the market.

He held all the cards to get Susan out of his life and Ro had given him most of them.

And that just pissed him off.

How had she, in such a short time, flipped his life inside out? Because of her, he'd started, just a little, to dream of accomplishments outside of his career, being a husband, having kids. Growing old with someone.

For the millionth time since leaving her alone at St. Urban he remembered that night, the pain in her deep, dark eyes.

After she'd spoken to Digby on the phone, he'd given her some time and space to process the reason for her adoption but when she hadn't returned home by dusk, he'd headed back to St. Urban, needing to see if she was okay.

On the drive over, he reluctantly admitted he was already in love with her and if she stuck around, happy to continue their no-commitment fling, he'd only fall deeper and deeper in love with her. And when she finally left—and she would, she'd told him she was only sticking around for another year—he'd fall into a bubbling, flesh-and-soul-stripping volcano.

He knew he should put distance between them, to create a barrier between them, but he couldn't leave her alone, not when she was upset and in pain. He'd try to be sensible later...if he could.

On arriving at St. Urban, he'd expected to find her crying but that wasn't the case. She sounded fine, *normal*, and the realization that she was talking to her ex had literally stopped him in his tracks.

He'd stood there out of her sight, trying to control his jealously. But then her words started to make sense. They said that eavesdroppers never heard anything good about themselves but Ro's honest and emotional declaration of how she felt nearly dropped him to the floor, in a good way. A bright, warm rush of love and a dose of happiness barreled through him and he'd hurried down the long veranda to get to her, prepared to yank the phone out of her hand and kiss her stupid...

She loved him, or something damn close to it.

Jack. Pot.

You're not good enough, you're unlovable, you're nothing...

Those long-ago phrases had him placing his hand on the wall, needing to steady himself.

What the hell are you thinking, Triple M? Have you lost your damn mind?

Terror immediately replaced tenderness. Love, he reminded himself, was the greatest weapon of all, dangerous because it lulled one into complacency before it proceeded to slice and dice you.

He'd thought his mother loved him, but she'd

shipped him off. Lu loved him, but she'd died. Susan pretended to love him in company and verbally annihilated him in private.

Muzi stared down at the wooden bar top, his eyes blurry with fatigue. Love confused and baffled him. He never knew which way was up. And that was why he avoided it.

And, Jesus, was it too much to ask for it to come with a guarantee or two?

"Hey, you're going to frighten my customers with your sour face," Pasco told him from the other side of the bar.

Muzi lifted his eyes and thought about asking Pasco for matches to prop open his eyelids. He hadn't slept and he was exhausted. But as soon as he closed his eyes, he started to think of Ro and how much he missed her. Unable to deal with that suck-fest, he moved on to thinking about Susan and her lifelong campaign of terror and all that did was increase the volume of noise in his head.

By tomorrow, at least one of those problems would be solved. But getting Ro out of his head and soul was going to require a lifetime of effort.

Pasco placed a drink in front of him and Muzi nearly gagged at the sight of a Bloody Mary. "I can't," he muttered, pushing the glass away.

Pasco pushed it back. "'You can and you will. And when you are done drinking that, you will go upstairs to my private apartment and take a long shower. I'll send some food up and then you will sleep."

Muzi heard the tough note in his voice and wondered whether he had the strength to argue. He didn't, so he picked up the Bloody Mary and downed it, trying not to gag.

"I'll go home, have a shower there and try to sleep," Muzi told Pasco, sliding off his barstool.

"Upstairs, *now*," Pasco ordered, sounding like Gordon Ramsay in a very bad mood.

He didn't have the energy to argue. "Yes, Chef." Muzi took a step toward a door marked Staff Only. He stopped, turned around and slid his hands into the pockets of his rumpled shorts.

"By the way, if you are serious about wanting to move back here, I heard that the owner of the Tempest-Vane trust is thinking about converting St. Urban into a luxurious boutique hotel and wants a restaurant on the premises. It might work for you."

Pasco's eyes widened in surprise. "That's *interesting*. I'd wondered why Ro was putting her heart and soul into restoring that wreck."

Muzi winced when he comprehended Pasco's meaning. "Pas, *crap*. How did you know?"

"I've got eyes, don't I? She and Digby are two peas in a pod."

Dammit. "You can't...don't...nobody is supposed to know."

Pasco looked him in the eye. "And nobody will. It's her secret to share, not mine." Muzi released his death grip on the doorframe. When Pasco gave his word, he never reneged on it.

"So, is she sticking around?"

"I don't know, you'd have to ask her," Muzi said, his tone bitter.

Pasco's eyebrows rose. "What the hell have you done, Muzi?"

"Why do you automatically assume it's my fault?" Muzi demanded, knowing that his tone lacked conviction.

"Because you're a moron," Pas replied. He rolled his eyes. "Go upstairs, shower, have a nap. When you've slept, things will look better."

Muzi rolled his eyes at him. "Sure they will."

He was completely sober, and his life looked pretty bleak.

Muzi was tempted, so tempted, to get drunk again.

Unbelievably, after a shower in Pasco's apartment upstairs, and a bowl of hearty chicken soup, Muzi stretched out on Pasco's long leather couch and drifted off to sleep. He woke six hours later, feeling...if not better, then more human.

After washing his face, he snagged some of Pasco's toothpaste and rubbed it over his teeth. He rinsed his mouth and stared at himself in the mirror, noticing his roadmap-like eyes and the gray pallor of his complexion. He needed to pull himself together and move the hell on.

But the thought of doing that without Ro made his stomach churn. How could he live his life without her in it? He lifted his chin and reminded himself that this wasn't his first rodeo: he'd survived after being separated from his mom, coped after Lu died.

He could do this. He *would*. But maybe he should go back to having shallow affairs with innocuous women. He ignored the thought that that was how his relationship with Ro began, with him thinking it was all about the sex.

It had been so, so much more. Ro was laughter and color, warmth and wit. She was the sunrise, her presence was the breaking of his night. She was midnight comfort, as her head used his shoulder for a pillow, his early morning jolt of energy, his reason for, well, everything...

Muzi placed his hands on the side of the basin and closed his eyes, sinking under the knowledge that she was everything to him. And that he'd let her go.

He knew, intellectually and through experience, that every day got a little easier, that heartbreak did eventually fade.

He hoped it faded before he did...

But, right now, he knew what he needed to do. He needed to go home, walk his lands and breathe in some warm, sultry air. When he'd done that, he'd spend some time working in his study and on something he could control, and that was work.

He could heal, he *would*. He just needed to be alone and to process the past few weeks. Everything would be fine in the end, he reminded himself, and if it wasn't fine, then it wasn't the end.

He entered the bar and saw that Pasco had been joined by Digby and, God, *Keane*. What the sodding hell? Standing in the doorway, he caught Pasco's eyes and scowled.

Pasco just motioned him over and nodded to an empty barstool to the left of Digby, who turned and gave him an up and down look. "So, you look like crap."

He knew that already. "What the hell are you doing here?" He growled the words, deliberately ignoring Keane.

Digby gestured to Pasco. "Dr. Phil here sent out an emergency SOS, telling us that you needed us, that you were falling apart."

Muzi considered wrapping his big hands around Pasco's neck, but settled for a threat. "I'm gonna kill you."

"You can try," Pasco told him, sliding a bottle of water across the bar.

Muzi, needing to do something with his hands, cracked the top. "And what the hell is he doing here?"

Muzi saw the long look Digby and Pasco exchanged. Digby, to his credit, was the first one to step onto the battlefield. "This cold war between you two has got to stop. We're tired of it."

Right now, Muzi didn't give a rat's ass about their feelings, he had too many of his own he was trying to corral. "He chose to believe the BS his mother has been spouting about me, about me running the business into the ground and stealing money from Clos du Cadieux."

Pasco and Digby both turned accusatory looks toward Keane. He lifted his hands and, to his credit, met Muzi's eyes. "Susan is a difficult woman and, with Rafe in the States, I'm all she has. In my defense, I didn't believe any of those wild claims."

"And yet you still walked away from me and our friendship," Muzi muttered, shocked at how much it still hurt. Keane abandoned him, just like his mom. And in a sense, like his grandmother did. Death was the ultimate abandonment wasn't it? Everyone he loved could, would and did, hurt him...

And that was why he ended it with Ro.

Keane rested his elbows on the table and pushed his hands into his hair. "Jesus, Triple M, I was *trying* to protect you. I always felt that, under her smiles, my mom didn't like you—"

Like... Such a small word for what she put him through.

"But her hatred of you bubbled over when we left university and joined Clos du Cadieux. And it went through the roof when Mimi appointed you as CEO."

"You're not telling me anything I don't know," Muzi pointed out.

"She told me to choose between her and you," Keane told him, his shoulders rising in agitation. "Honestly, I would've chosen you. But Susan is a basket case and, with Rafe leaving, I knew that if I sided with you, there would be no one to curtail her worst impulses. When Mimi retired, she told the family that she didn't want to hear of any squabbling at Clos du Cadieux. I am the only one who can talk sense into Susan, to make her consider her actions. I sided with her to protect you!"

"I don't need protecting!" Muzi said, his voice rising.

"From Susan you do," Keane insisted. "She hates you—she always has. Looking back, I think I've only just realized how much."

Muzi didn't want to think about that, didn't want to acknowledge the guilt and sorrow in his brother's eyes. The past couldn't be changed.

"So, you detonated our friendship to protect me?" Muzi scoffed.

Keane looked him in the eye. "Yeah, I did. Susan has had some wild schemes over the years concerning you but I, mostly, managed to deflect her."

"So why are you telling me this now?" Muzi demanded. "Why are you here?"

"Because when I get a message telling me that your life is falling apart and that Pas has never seen you so defeated, I will always come running," Keane told him, his voice strong and sure. "My mother is mad but you, *you* are my brother."

Muzi felt the prickle of tears at his sincerity, still trying to wrap his head around what he was hearing. "You could've come to me and told me what you were doing, Keane. Losing you…" He couldn't continue, it hurt too much.

Keane placed a hand on his shoulder and squeezed. "I know, I'm sorry. It was just supposed to be for a few months, but the gap I created just kept getting wider and wider until I didn't know how to bridge it. Can you forgive me, Triple M? I *am* damn sorry."

Before they got to that point, there was something

else Keane should know. "I'm going to bury your mother tomorrow at the board meeting."

Keane's expression remained inscrutable, but curiosity jumped into his eyes. "How?" he asked, his tone careful.

Muzi, knowing that he was taking the risk that Keane would take what he was about to say straight to Susan, explained his plan and Keane nodded. Muzi held his breath, waiting for his response. "I think that's a perfect plan. The board will vote to keep you."

"You think?"

Keane nodded. "Trust me, there have been rumblings for a while that Susan's animosity toward you is hindering rather than helping the situation. I have been asked to persuade her to retire."

Muzi felt one of the many boulders sitting on his chest roll away.

"The board, and I, will all vote for you," Keane told him. He lifted his glass of whiskey, sipped, and Muzi saw regret and fear roll across his face. "I messed up, and I'm tired of being on the outside of your life. Can we...is there any chance..."

His words trailed off but Muzi knew what he was asking. Could they go back? Could they try again? Could they repair their relationship? It would take time, effort but...yeah. He thought they could. Because he did, somewhere where truth resided, believe that Keane had been trying to look after his best interests.

He nodded and held out his hand for Keane to

shake. Keane took it a step further by pulling him into a one-armed hug.

"Cut it out, you're acting like two overly emotional teenage girls!" Pasco broke the soppy moment with his sarcastic quip but Muzi could see that he was pleased. As was Digby.

Muzi raised his bottle, thinking he needed something stronger. "Can I have something with alcohol in it?" he asked Pasco.

"Hell, no," Pasco told him, pulling the whiskey bottle out of his reach. "You still have work to do, my friend."

Muzi lifted his hands, confused. "What work?"

"My sister," Digby stated, his tone hard.

Ah, crap. He might've regained one friend, but, judging by Digby's face, he might be losing another. He looked for something to say, found nothing and opted to keep his mouth shut.

"What? No explanation?" Digby demanded.

"I'm not sure what you need me to explain," Muzi carefully replied.

"Well, according to Bay and Brinley, my sister is currently sleeping at St. Urban because you kicked her out of your place. And your bed, and your life."

True. He didn't need to be a rocket scientist to know that Radd and Digby's women were not impressed with him.

"I should take you outside and pummel the hell out of you," Digby muttered.

That was okay with Muzi, he needed an outlet for

his stress and he couldn't possibly feel worse than he already did.

"Why did you kick her out? Especially after she was ambushed by the truth of her adoption?" Keane asked him, ignoring Digby.

Hell, did everyone now know who Ro was, her real connection to Radd and Digby? She was going to eviscerate him when she found out. With a blunt teaspoon. He threw up his hands and scowled at Digby, who winced.

"I told Keane," Digby admitted. "Pasco worked it out for himself."

"If either of you tells anyone, I will break you," Muzi told Keane and Pasco. They wouldn't but a strong warning was warranted.

Muzi shook his head, feeling like he'd stepped into a world where nothing made sense. "I gave her time to be alone, as she asked. When I returned, she was on the phone with her idiot ex."

"If you are about to tell us that she's still in love with him, I will deck you," Digby threatened.

"No, she told him about us...that she's this close—" Muzi held up his thumb and index finger an inch apart "—to falling in love with me."

All three faces reflected confusion. "And that's a problem?" Digby asked.

"Yes! The way we feel about each other is crazy! It's insane, intense, intimidating!"

"Incredible, irrational... I can't think of any more words starting with an *i*," Pasco drawled.

Muzi had the feeling that Pasco was taking the

piss. When he had the energy, he would make him pay for that remark.

Muzi thought he'd try, once again, to explain. He didn't hold out much hope that they'd get it. "Look, we have the power to hurt each other, badly. I'm not thrilled at being in that position but, worse than that, I couldn't live with myself if *I* hurt *her*."

Digby lifted his beer bottle to his lips and took a long swallow. "So don't hurt her, half-wit."

"Poor Ro, she's had a tough few days—ambushed by her ex and dumped by the man she's crazy about," Pasco mused. "I should go and comfort her."

"Only if you want to be buried in a shallow grave," Muzi growled.

"I should kick your ass for sleeping with her and then treating her like crap, man," Digby told him, and Muzi saw his bunched fists.

"It wasn't like that… I didn't…" God, he was a reasonably erudite man, why couldn't he find any words today? He stood up, reached across the bar, grabbed the whiskey bottle and took a slug. He felt the burn down his throat and, resting the bottle against his forehead, groaned.

"In my defense, it was a crazy day. I thought—assumed—that she was going back to the States. A little earlier she told me that she was going to stick around for another six months, maybe a year, and I was happy, I thought I had time to persuade her to stay forever. But then, hours later, she hits me with the possibility of love and forever and trying for more…and… God… I…"

"Take another belt, Triple M," Pasco suggested.

Muzi took another sip of whiskey and passed it back to Pasco, who put it under the counter, out of his reach. "She terrifies me. What I feel for her scares the hell out of me," he finally admitted.

Digby nodded, looking satisfied. "Good, it should scare you. Love is terrifying but that's no reason to run from it."

"Yeah, *that*," Pasco said, pointing his beer bottle at Muzi.

"Shut up, Kildare, you only have one-night stands and have no idea what you are talking about," Digby told him.

Digby turned his intense gaze, his eyes the same color as Ro's, on him. "Falling for someone is a big deal and it should cause your breath to hitch and your heart to stop. Look, you can carry on being a coward or you can face that fear. Step into the unknown and trust that the way you feel for each other, that the love you have for each other, your desire not to mess up and hurt each other, is enough to carry you through.

"I've never known you to be a coward, Triple M," Digby said, his voice silky with challenge.

God, was he trying to dare him into a relationship with his sister? And was he tempted? He was. He really was.

"I didn't expect or plan on her. I never expected to feel this way."

"We all think we can control what we feel but, when the right woman comes along, we're bowled over," Digby said. "Radd did, I did, it looks like you have too, M."

"I didn't mean to," Muzi grumbled.

"Neither did any of us," Digby cheerfully replied before his expression sobered. "But what I can't forget is that my sister is alone in an old, huge house, probably crying her eyes out because you are a cowardly dipstick. So, are you going to do something about that, about *her*?"

Doing something meant telling her how he felt, asking for another chance, telling her that he wanted so much more than he ever had. It meant putting his heart into her hands, taking a chance.

Being brave.

"At the risk of repeating myself, love is scary, Muzi. Terrifying, actually," Digby told him, his voice vibrating with emotion. "It's hard, but so is being alone, so is not having her in your life. Choose your hard, Triple M."

CHAPTER ELEVEN

CHOOSE YOUR HARD...

Muzi thought about Digby's words as he drove over to St. Urban. It was fully dark and his headlights cut through the night, showing him only the next few yards of the road.

But that was okay, he didn't need to see hundreds of yards ahead, he just needed to navigate what he could see.

It was, he realized, a metaphor for life. He couldn't see into the future, there were no guarantees that Ro wouldn't die or disappear, but that was far in the future, shrouded in darkness. He needed to navigate life as it was in front of him, the few yards he could see.

If he wanted Ro, and he did, he needed to live a little more in the present. The past, as Mimi often declared, was a memory and the future was imagination. Only the here and now mattered.

And Ro mattered most of all.

Because he didn't want to scare her—and because he wasn't a complete moron—Muzi texted Ro to tell her he was on his way. But his warning would also give her the chance to avoid him and he hoped he didn't have to start chasing her all over the country. Or the world.

He would but it would be a pain in the ass.

Muzi pulled up in front of the steps leading up to the front door, his headlights catching the small figure sitting on the wall, dressed in a pair of skimpy shorts and a cropped T-shirt. Her long hair hung down in waves and even in that glance he had, he could see her pinched face, her wide eyes.

Her wariness.

He shut down the car, climbed out, and kept his eyes on her as he walked over the gravel drive and up the steps. As his eyes became accustomed to the darkness, he saw her pull her knees up to her chest, her pose defensive.

"What do you want?" she demanded.

He stopped a short distance from her but close enough to realize that she'd recently showered and that her long hair was still wet. And that her eyes were red from crying.

He thought about how to respond to questions and decided that he might as well start with what was important.

"You. I want *you*."

Ro, her heart thundering in her chest, heard his simple statement and stared up at him, not knowing what to say or how to react. What did that even mean?

How did he want her? In bed, up against a wall?

As a fling, his partner or a significant other? Did he want her for now, for the next few months, or forever?

Why did men have to always skimp on the details?

"I think you need to explain that statement," Ro carefully told him.

Muzi nodded, crossed his arms and widened his stance. He looked big, powerful and intimidating but, even in the low light—the moon wasn't quite as bright as it had been—she could see the emotion roiling beneath his surface. It was in his eyes, in his tense jaw, in the way his nostrils flared every couple of seconds.

He didn't speak and she didn't know how to broach the subject of their relationship—or current lack thereof—so Ro broke their silence by telling him that she'd taken a walk in the vineyard the night before.

Muzi frowned. "I'm not crazy about you walking the lands alone at night."

Ro waved his concern away. "I was on a video call to my folks—and yes, they are still divorcing—"

"And how do you feel about that?"

Fine. Better than fine. "They explained that they still love each other but that their love has changed. They are still the best of friends and still plan to stay in each other's lives so there won't be any awkwardness or taking of sides. I'm grateful for that. And, of course, they still love me as much as they ever did."

Muzi's mouth lifted in that sexy half smile she so loved. "Of course they do."

Ro waved her hands in the air. "But that's not what I wanted to tell you. So, I was sitting there, in between the vines on the east side of the property where your guys have been working. And I was watching the moonlight on the vine leaves and, you're going to think I'm crazy, but I think I might've found your cultivar. I saw some distinct differences…"

His expression didn't change and Ro frowned. "Why aren't you happy about this?"

Muzi shrugged. "I am, I guess. But, honestly, the C'Artegan cultivar is way down on my list of important stuff right now."

Oh, man, this was bad. If Muzi wasn't reacting to her news about finding the cultivar he was desperately looking for, then their night was going to go downhill fast.

She took a deep breath and forced herself to verbalize her thoughts. "Then what's at the top of that list?"

Muzi sat down on the wall next to her and stretched out his long legs.

"Did you not hear me say that I want you?" Muzi asked, his tone gentle. He sighed and linked his hands behind his head. "God, could I be any worse at this if I tried?"

Before she could reply—not that she had a response to his rhetorical question—he spoke again. "Let me back up a bit and start with this… I'm so sorry you were hurt when you found out what Gil and Zia did," Muzi quietly stated. "I thought you could handle the truth. But, in hindsight, maybe I should've protected you from that knowledge."

"You were right to tell me, and the last of my illusions have fallen away. In my head, they are sperm and egg donors but not my parents." Ro put her hand on her heart and smiled. "My parents are pretty damn wonderful, actually."

"I'm sure they are. They raised an incredible woman."

His words washed over her, but they weren't enough, she needed more. "What are we doing, Muzi? Where is this conversation going?"

Muzi pulled his thigh up onto the wall and turned to face her, his expression pensive. "I didn't plan for you, Roisin, I didn't plan for *this*. I was quite happy to be alone, content to have the occasional affair. I convinced myself that I didn't need anybody, that love wasn't worth the risk.

"And that I don't need anybody..." Muzi added.

Ro's heart, which had started to soar, stalled and plummeted back down to earth.

"But I do need *you*," Muzi said, his voice rough with emotion. "I know that you are still recovering from being in a long-term relationship, that another relationship might not be what you want but I'll be here—I'll take anything you can give me—hoping that you will love me the way I love you."

Ah...*what?*

"You love me?" Ro squeaked.

Muzi rubbed the back of his neck, looking uncomfortable. "I wish what I felt for you was that simple.

Yes, I love you but it's more than that." He hesitated and Ro held her breath, unable to catch her heart, which was on a death-defying roller-coaster ride.

"I've fallen into you…into a dream of a future we can have together. I can see us creating a life together, living and loving together, creating babies and memories." He managed a small smile, moonlight in his eyes. "I've been scared before—scared that I'd be alone, abandoned by Mimi and the family—but losing you, it's a level of fear that can drop me to my knees. *You* drop me to my knees…" Muzi added.

She wanted to reach for him, to tell him that she wanted what he did, but there was something she had to get out first.

"We both want, or wanted, guarantees that our hearts would be safe, that we won't hurt each other but—" Ro hesitated, emotion closing her throat. She pushed the words past the tightness, and they came out a little rough. "But as I've recently discovered, love doesn't come with a guarantee."

"I *know*. And it's so damn terrifying," Muzi said, his hand coming to rest on her bare foot. "The thing is Ro, I'll take you, I'll take whatever you can give me. I choose you without any guarantee. That's true right now and I have to believe that it'll be true tomorrow and ten years, twenty, from now."

His thumb brushed the instep of her foot and heat rolled up her leg. She lifted her head and stared at him, unable to believe that this reticent man was saying exactly what she most needed to hear.

That he loved her, that he wanted her in his life…

"Put me out of my misery and tell me that I have a chance, Ro," Muzi begged. "Stay here with me, create a life with me."

Ro nodded and knew her smile was tremulous. "Okay," she whispered.

Muzi bent his head toward her. "Sorry, I didn't hear that?"

Oh, he absolutely did, the man had excellent hearing. Ro's smile grew stronger. "Yes, Muzi. Yes, to the life and babies and the vines and living in your house. But mostly yes to loving you. As hard as I can…"

Muzi closed his eyes and rested his forehead on her bent knees. "Thank God."

Ro kissed the top of his head, and when he lifted his face to look at her, she kissed his lips, unable to stop her smile. "I'm so insanely, wonderfully, utterly in love with you."

Muzi clasped her face in his big hands. "And I you." He stared at her and at that moment, the brief slice of time before his lips met hers, the world stopped and they were the only two people on earth, standing under a suddenly bright moon. Anticipation danced between them and she waited, not wanting the intense, powerful moment to end…

Then he kissed her, and she realized that it wasn't the end but simply the beginning.

Ro pulled back and sent him a cheeky smile. "Want to take a walk and look at the C'Artegan vines?"

Muzi stood up and scooped her up, cradling her against his big chest. "Again, not anywhere near the top of my 'Things that are most important right now' list."

Ro sighed, linked her arm around his neck and kissed his jaw, and he strode into the house. She did not doubt that she was priority one on that list, just as he was on hers.

And they'd both work damn hard, for the rest of their lives, to keep it that way.

* * * * *

If you didn't want
How to Tempt the Off-Limits Billionaire
to end make sure you catch the first
and second installments in the
South Africa's Scandalous Billionaires trilogy!

How to Undo the Proud Billionaire
How to Win the Wild Billionaire

COMING NEXT MONTH FROM

PRESENTS

#3953 HIS MAJESTY'S HIDDEN HEIR
Princesses by Royal Decree
by Lucy Monroe
Prince Konstantin can't forget Emma Carmichael, the woman who
vanished after royal pressure forced him to end their relationship.
A surprise meeting five years later shocks Konstantin: Emma has a
son. Unmistakably *his* son. And now he'll claim them both!

#3954 THE GREEK'S CINDERELLA DEAL
Cinderellas of Convenience
by Carol Marinelli
When tycoon Costa declares he'll hire Mary if she attends a party
with him, she's dazed—by his generosity and their outrageous
attraction! And as the clock strikes midnight on their deal,
Cinderella unravels—in the Greek's bed...

#3955 PREGNANT AFTER ONE FORBIDDEN NIGHT
The Queen's Guard
by Marcella Bell
Innocent royal guard Jenna has never been tempted away
from duty. She's never been tempted by a man before! Until her
forbidden night with notoriously untamable billionaire Sebastian,
which ends with her carrying his baby!

#3956 THE BRIDE HE STOLE FOR CHRISTMAS
by Caitlin Crews
Hours before the woman he can't forget walks down the aisle,
Crete steals Timoney back! And now he has the night before
Christmas to prove to them both that he won't break her heart all
over again...

HPCNMRA1021

#3957 BOUND BY HER SHOCKING SECRET
by Abby Green

It takes all of Mia's courage to tell tycoon Daniel about their daughter. Though tragedy tore them apart, he deserves to know he's a father. But accepting his proposal? That will require something far more extraordinary...

#3958 CONFESSIONS OF HIS CHRISTMAS HOUSEKEEPER
by Sharon Kendrick

Stunned when an accident leaves her estranged husband, Giacomo, unable to remember their year-long marriage, Louise becomes his temporary housekeeper. She'll spend Christmas helping him regain his memory. But dare she confess the explosive feelings she still has for him?

#3959 UNWRAPPED BY HER ITALIAN BOSS
Christmas with a Billionaire
by Michelle Smart

After a rocky first impression, innocent Meredith's got a lot to prove to her new billionaire boss, Giovanni! He's trusting her to make his opulent train's maiden voyage a success. Trusting herself around him? That's another challenge entirely...

#3960 THE BILLIONAIRE'S PROPOSITION IN PARIS
Secrets of Billionaire Siblings
by Heidi Rice

By hiring event planner Katherine and inviting her to a lavish Paris ball, Connall plans to find out all he needs to take revenge on her half brother. He's not counting on their ever-building electricity to bring him to his knees!

YOU CAN FIND MORE INFORMATION ON UPCOMING HARLEQUIN TITLES, FREE EXCERPTS AND MORE AT HARLEQUIN.COM.

HPCNMRB1021